Percy & the Plod

Book Number One in the
Percy Veerance Adventure Series

Percy & the Plod

Toni Dockter

Illustrated by Amy Smith and Tonette Twonky
Cover Illustration by Catherine Jampierre

FWE Publishing
Soquel,
California

Percy & the Plod is published by

Fuchsia Woman Enterprises Publishing.

Percy Veerance™ and Plod On™ are registered trademarks.

ISBN 0-9712201-0-7

Second edition

Library of Congress Catalog Number 2001119463

PRINTED IN THE UNITED STATES OF AMERICA

This book is dedicated to:

TWONKY ZOTZ

mi chimpy amoré

And to struggling writers everywhere:

Write On!

Acknowledgments

Thanks for the continued support:
William Buckley
Claire Daschbach
Roger Dockter
Lorrie Gnos
Scott Zimmer

Thanks for the encouragement:
Robert L. Baker, Judi Barton, Leah Daschbach,
Pav and Joe Meyer, Marie Parker

Thanks for the editing and proofreading:
Vanessa Rennard, Kalei O'Sullivan
Sharon Young, Karen Pershing, Joan Phelps

Thanks for the graphics and artwork:
Marti Bercaw

Thanks for the book production:
Janice Phelps

Thanks for the website:
Kim Dumas

Awe and appreciation to:
Lewis Carroll, Emily Dickinson, Ralph Waldo Emerson, Robert Frost, Rudyard Kipling,
Henry Wadsworth Longfellow, Edna St. Vincent Millay, Edgar Allan Poe, William
Shakespeare, Dylan Thomas, and Walt Whitman

Table of Contents

Land of Yoosa

NOT SO LONG AGO AND NOT SO FAR AWAY, Yoosa was a land of beauty and light. Amber plains and emerald hills stretched far and wide. Throughout the countryside, sapphire streams flowed. Every day the sun sparkled like a brilliant topaz. Every night the stars flickered like diamonds. Towering over the land like a purple pyramid was Yoosa's crown jewel, Amethyst Mountain. Yoosians revered the mountain, keeper of the sun. Tethered by a rope at the peak, the sun revolved around Yoosa all day long, like clockwork. In fact, Yoosians could set their watches by the sun's position over the mountain.

So, too, was Yoosa a land of plenty, with plenty of farms. Everyone farmed, each farmer a specialist. For instance, one farmer grew straw, while another grew chickens; one grew pancakes, another horseflies, and so forth. There were large farms, like the Bovine meat farm and the Xotic fruit and jam farm. Medium-sized farms produced things like cottage cheese, books, pillows and quilts, bricks, wooden furniture, and tombstones. But the majority of farms were small, like the ones that made cappuccinos, sequins, pencils, hair curlers, music, hat racks, crackers, fancy underwear, veggie pops, Scoot Boots (popular with kids), mushroom juice (popular with older folks), poetry (not popular with anyone), and junk. Anything a person could want was home grown in Yoosa.

Yoosians used the barter system. Traded for what they needed. They were prosperous folks. Even the dental floss farmer made a good living.

Yoosians were content. And content with each other. Sure, one could find a quirky person here, an irksome person there. In a population that size, there was bound to be a malcontent from time to time. But no one kept count. Yoosians avoided conflict. Every generation planned to live happily ever after. How could anything go wrong?

But something did. One day the sun started to fade. No one knew why. Each day fewer minutes of sunlight shone on the countryside. At first, Yoosians paid little attention. They offered explanations: "The sun is recharging itself," or "The sun is resting." And the most popular theory: "The sun is on vacation, fishing and boating at a lake." Everyone needs a vacation, they thought. They also thought the sun would be back soon, bright and sunny as always.

Unfortunately, this did not happen. As time went on, the sunlight condition worsened. Fewer minutes turned into fewer hours. Yoosa's pleasant environment was threatened. People feared for their future. If the sun left forever, what would they do? How could they live?

As sunlight diminished, the atmosphere changed. So did people's moods. For the first time ever, Yoosians spent more time at Dreary Lake than Cheery Lake. As the days grew darker, niceness grew shorter. Spontaneous rudeness erupted, like name calling ("Get off my property, Needle-Nose Nelson, you pointy-nose son of a Nels!"), cutting in line at the Farmer's Fair to trade for Farmer Sushiyama's carp-flavored toothpaste, or forgetting to say "Pardon me" when someone ran over someone else in his buggy. Similarly, another phenomenon emerged: arguing. Yoosians now argued over anything—like which day of the week should be trash day, or who had the biggest farm, or whether it was okay to sing in the rain.

Without the sun, sadness grew. There were no more smiles at the Happy Clown Farm. The poetry farmer wept over the loss of sunsets. Odd behavior developed as well, like wall-wailing—sitting on a fence and moaning about things such as toenails or baloney sandwiches. Trading, too, became wacky—such as a farmer trying to trade a toothpick for a wagon—or a peach pit for a cow. Or refusing to trade at all.

Yoosa was falling apart! Something had to be done. But what? A coalition of Yoosians turned to their elected official, Mayor Oscar, for help. They begged him to find an answer to the sun problem. The mayor's office was in turmoil trying to control the outbreak of wailing and appease a group of citizens who had asked the mayor to construct a bridge they could jump from.

Mayor Oscar stated that he was an elected official, not a wizard and, therefore, had no solutions. However, since an election year was approaching, he reversed his position on the issue. He conferred with the wisest consultant in Yoosa–Lasco, the Tree of Knowledge. Lasco knew exactly what the problem was. The Tree waved its branches and tossed a cluster of wisdom fruit into the air. The fruit landed on the ground in a configuration of words and punctuation. The mayor read the fruity sentence aloud: "The sun is drifting away because someone on top of the mountain is untying the rope."

This is where Percy's story begins.

One

♫ Percy and Dilly

WITH HIS HANDS, FACE, AND GLASSES covered in dirt, Percy toiled in a field of turnips, using his own system to harvest vegetables. He had invented it a year ago after his aunt gave him a book about science for his tenth birthday. He called it the "Scientific Calculating Method," applicable to all vegetables. Here's how it worked: first, Percy examined the stalks or leaves for texture and hue. Then he measured them with a pocket ruler. Then he used a self-made chart to compute which produce was the ideal color, size, and shape. Lastly, he picked. Percy was thorough, as harvesting vegetables was a serious job for him. He wanted to pick only the best because his dad was a picky farmer. Besides, the better the vegetables, the better the real food they could be traded for. Like meat loaf.

All morning Percy inspected, pulled, and sorted turnips. When he finished a row, he clapped his hands, then whistled to his dog, Dilly. Percy relied on Dilly's help in the field. Dilly was great at using his paws like flippers. He batted the vegetables into neat piles so Percy could bag them quickly.

"Here, Dilly!" Percy yelled across the rows. "Time to stack!"

At that minute, Dilly had other plans. Swift as a missile, he jetted after a gopher. His body was aerodynamically efficient—cucumber shaped, tailless, stumpy but powerful legs. Percy knew the gopher hadn't a chance. He smiled as Dilly chased the gopher up the pole of the "Veerance Family Farm" sign. The gopher hid in the cutout of the letter "V." A stolen turnip dangled from its mouth.

"Ruff!" Dilly pawed at the sign and shook it. The gopher fell from the sign and fled. Dilly sprinted after it. As he did, the glasses on his snout bounced up and down. People said Percy and Dilly looked alike because they both had brown hair and glasses. They said that when they walked together, Dilly's ears flopped up and down on his head the same way as Percy's cowlick flopped up and down.

Percy fell in love with Dilly the first time he saw him on his grandpap's cricket farm. Unlike the other puppies in the litter, Dilly was born with an elongated body covered with fuzz instead of fur. Where his tail should have been was a lump instead. Grandpap Gence said he had never seen anything like it before. "Must have been all the gherkins his mother ate when she was pregnant."

"I think he's a beaut!" Percy said.

"He's as healthy as a cricket, except one thing—his vision. He keeps bumping into things. But he's unique, I can say that. Like you, Percy."

"Could I have him, Grandpap? Please? Could I?" Percy asked.

Grandpa Gence laughed. "If anyone would want this funny-looking mutt, it would be you, Percy."

"I promise to feed him and take excellent care of him."

"What will your folks say?"

"They won't care. Besides, I'll teach him to help me with my farm chores."

"Will you get him a good pair of spectacles?"

"Sure, I will. I know what it's like not to see good."

"At the eyeglasses farm, tell Farmer Klops that his ol' buddy Telly sent you. He'll give you a good deal."

Percy picked up his new puppy and hugged him. They bumped noses.

"What are you going to name him?" asked Grandpap Gence.

"He looks like a pickle. I'm naming him Dilly."

After Dilly had scared the gopher away, he dashed back through the fields. He leapt into Percy's arms, knocking him over on his back. Percy lay sprawled on the ground. He held up a giant turnip for Dilly to see. "Look how big this one is! Dad will be so happy."

"Ruff!"

Percy rolled over on his stomach and inhaled the rich scent of the earth. The smell soothed him. Something squiggled next to his face. He jumped to his feet. His cowlick stuck up like an arrow.

Dilly lunged at the squiggle and caught a slimy worm between his teeth.

"Eewww," Percy said. "Get that away from me!"

Dilly whipped his head back and forth. The worm broke in half. Each piece slithered off in a different direction.

"Good boy, Dilly." Percy could always count on Dilly to protect him. Dilly was a great dog.

Percy heard wheels rattle. In the distance, he saw his dad, Vance Veerance, sitting at the reins of their horse-drawn cart. He steered toward them, or at least tried to. Mona, the roan-colored mare, shuffled along. "Giddy up, gal!" Mr. Veerance said. Mona looked back and whinnied.

Percy was fond of Mona, even if she was the sorriest animal he had ever seen—swayback, patchy hair, buckteeth, sad disposition, and slow. When Mr. Veerance bartered with Bronco Snozhead, the horse trader farmer, he said he hadn't noticed Mona's curved back, crooked legs, or droopy eyes. Mona cost Mr. Veerance a dozen cases of vegetables and a stack of his prized six-foot-tall carrots, which prompted him to tell Percy, "Egads! Never trade with a horse trader!" And he never did again.

Mr. Veerance's aversion to horse traders transferred to other animal traders, like the Bovines, the cattle farmers (their meat farm was the largest in Yoosa); the Ewings who were sheep farmers; and the Malatetes, the pig farmers. Hence, little meat for the Veerance family. Percy loved bacon, but he was glad his dad didn't want to trade with Mo'e Malatete. His kids, Mo'poke and Mo'reen, were twin snout-nosed mini-thugs who started picking on him ever since the sun started to fade. Percy was also glad his mom turned down the annual invitation to the Malatete Swine Soiree and Pork Rind Fest. She said it sounded too greasy. His dad said pigs' feet were not made to eat.

Percy wasn't pleased about the loss of trade with the Bovines, steak being one of his favorite foods. And he would miss trading with the Ewings and visiting their farm. He liked to see cute Mary Ewing. She cared for her pet lamb, Queenie, the same way he cared for Dilly. Mary and Queenie had the same curly hair. Whenever Percy had gone to the Ewing farm, he'd wanted to say "Hi" to Mary. So far he hadn't been brave enough, but one day....

❋ ❋ ❋

Percy watched Mona saunter toward them and knew his dad was losing patience with her by the minute. The only time Mona had shown any spunk was when she pranced by the Kismet's farm. She had a crush on Spotty Kismet's piebald horse, Geldinger. But Geldinger was no stud. He paid no attention to Mona, causing her to neigh all the way home. Percy felt bad for her.

It was Percy's job to brush Mona, but she never cantered enough to work up a lather. Her hair was so sparse that Percy settled for combing it gently around her face—which made Mona snort, a habit Dilly picked up.

Even from a distance, Mona looked pitiful. Percy reminded himself to bring her more straw and extra oats for dinner. Also in the distance, his father's orange hair was hard to miss. His head looked like it was covered in orange peel. "Dad's coming," Percy said to Dilly. "Help me bag the turnips."

At the turnip field, Mr. Veerance pulled on Mona's reins. She moaned and stopped. He climbed from the wagon. Chewing on a carrot stick, he held up the first sack of turnips. "Not very heavy. How are you picking them, Percy?"

"One by one," Percy said.

"Next time, grab two at a time."

"Look at this big one, Dad." Percy held up the giant turnip. "Isn't it a beaut?"

"Next time, try to pick more. Hop in, we're leaving," Mr. Veerance said. "Hyaw, hyaw, move it, Mona!"

The mare bared her large teeth and lomped along. Percy cleaned his glasses on his shirt. From the back pocket of his overalls, he pulled out a book and flipped open the pages of *The Flamboyant Flamingo.*

His dad gave Percy a sideways glance. "You've been reading that same book for weeks."

"I know," Percy said. "I like to read slow. Makes the story last longer."

"Where'd you get the book?"

"Auntie Flora gave it to me."

"Why?"

"Because I like to read. She gives me lots of books. She says books are the keys to the universe."

"Your aunt says a lot of things. Where'd she get the book?"

"She trades with the book farmer."

"The book farmer wants to trade for flowers? Egads! Don't end up like that." Mr. Veerance shook his head. "Besides, you should be playing with the other kids instead of reading all the time."

Percy kept his head down and continued to read. He didn't have much time to play—too many vegetables to pick in the summer season. Even if there was more time to play, the other kids didn't want to play with him (which Percy wasn't about to tell his dad).

"And another thing, Percy. You should build up your muscles. You're awfully skinny. I wasn't like that when I was twelve years old. I had meat on my bones."

Maybe *next year* when he would be twelve, and maybe if he got to eat more meat, he could store it on his bones and get bigger.

"Dad, can we trade turnips for raspberries? They're in season at the

Xotic Fruit Farm. Mr. Dent traded a spool of dental floss for a big basket. He said they're really toothsome."

Mr. Veerance jiggled Mona's reins. She moved slower instead of faster. "I can't understand why the fruit farm does more business than our farm. That farm is getting bigger all the time—and ours isn't."

"Look at it this way, Dad," Percy said. "Which would you rather eat—a strawberry or a lima bean?"

Mr. Veerance looked at his son with a serious face. "A lima bean, of course."

Percy should have known.

"How about if I show you how to swat flies tonight?" Mr. Veerance said. He waved one arm around like a sword-fighter. "Everyone says I've developed championship form."

"No, thanks, Dad," Percy said quietly. He wanted to finish reading his book.

A dark cloud passed over the sun, the sky grew more dim. Even though it was a summer afternoon, there was barely enough light to read. Percy frowned. "What are we going to do about the sun, Dad?"

"Nothing," Mr. Veerance said. "We're going home. I'm hungry."

Two

✦ The Veerance Family

I N A CORNER OF THE KITCHEN, Percy's mom stirred vegetables in a pot on a wood-burning stove. In the middle of the room, a thick plank of wood rested on four tree stumps. The plank served as a table, a workbench, a cutting board, a canning station, and most importantly for Mrs. Veerance, the counter for her laboratory. She considered herself a Vegetable Cuisine Scientist. She signed her name as "Vera Veerance, V.C.S." Daily, she experimented with recipes for her family.

Percy sat on a stool at the plank table while Dilly snoozed at his feet. He could smell his mom's latest creation—flambéed curried beets. It made his cowlick quiver. He wished beets had never been invented. Even more, he wished his mother's recipes had never been invented.

On his lap, he held his baby sister, Peggie. She had a dimple in her chin and a long tuft of hair at the center of her egg-shaped head. (Maybe the start of a cowlick?) Percy thought Peg looked like a chubby sparrow. And like a little bird, she tilted her head back, opened her mouth, and waited for Percy to spoon peas into it. She swallowed without chewing, then opened her mouth again, over and over. Peg loved vegetables, especially peas, which baffled Percy. "Dad, will Peg turn green if she eats too many peas?"

Mr. Veerance worked intently on the other side of the plank table, hollowing out a stack of zucchini . Chewing on a carrot stick, he gave Percy a look. He mashed some zucchini pulp, added a sprig of spearmint to the mix. "Her head might get pea-shaped," he said. He then squished the mixture into a zucchini tube and squeezed a drop onto his finger and licked it. "Mmmm, a new batch of toothpaste! Taste it, Vera."

"Delicious!" Mrs. Veerance said. "Vance, you should trade your toothpaste at the Farmer's Fair. Yours is better than Clara Clumpie's cottage cheese brand. Too many lumps. And I don't like Farmer Sushiyama's carp-flavored toothpaste at all!"

Percy cringed, remembering when his dad had traded Mayor Oscar for his "Leftovers-Flavored Toothpaste" (made with scraps from the mayor's sausage, sauerkraut, and baloney farm). Percy refused to brush with it, saying he'd rather have his teeth turn brown and fall out.

"Mo' mo' mo'," Peg said.

Percy shoveled a spoonful of peas into her gaping mouth and looked over at his mother. "Mom, do you know how to make roast beef?"

"Oh, Percy, I didn't see you there."

"I've been here the whole time."

"You must blend in with the furniture, dear."

Which furniture? The stools? Percy's cowlick stuck up. Mrs. Veerance continued stirring. Mr. Veerance filled another zucchini tube. Peg swallowed peas. Percy waited. "Well, Mom?"

"Well, what?

"Can you cook roast beef?"

"For what?"

"To eat. Like for dinner."

"Oh, I've made something much better. Spinach and curried beet casserole. It's a beautiful color." She handed Percy a plateful.

"Eeeee," squealed Peg.

Percy attempted to eat one bite. It was as awful tasting as he'd thought. He secretly spit the half-chewed mouthful into his napkin. "Do we always have to have vegetables?"

Mrs. Veerance began to sing, which was her second favorite thing to do after experimental cooking. (She composed original songs in an instant—anytime, anywhere. Percy could never figure out what inspired her.)

Eat your veggies. They're so good.
Eat your veggies like you know you should. Tra la la la la

Dilly woke up startled and banged his head on the stool leg. Percy looked down and saw Dilly cover his ears with his paws. Percy wanted to cover his ears, too.

Mrs. Veerance continued with gusto:

Vegetables make you big and strong
Everybody sing along La la la la la...

Percy ate plenty of vegetables. He didn't feel big and strong. He finished feeding his sister and put her in a playpen next to the warm oven.

"No milk, or shirts, or eggs, or straw for Mona's stall, or candles, or bricks, or soap, or horseflies for awhile," Mr. Veerance said. He said "horseflies" with a sadness in his voice. He traded extensively with the horsefly farmer, No Lips Barney. Mr. Veerance liked to sit on the porch in the evening and swat flies. His record was 113 in one night. His goal was 150. "The other farmers are getting too stingy."

"Why?" asked Percy.

"The darned sun. Since it started drifting away, the farmers are scared. Think they have to hoard products. We'll have to make do without their wares, and them without ours. We'll just see how Yoosians like to be without vegetables—ha!"

"No bananas or apples either, Dad?"

"NO!"

Percy didn't have to ask about T-bones or lamb chops.

"I found a substitute for milk," Mrs. Veerance said. "I traded with Mrs. Yin for mushroom juice. Used it in my tea. Murky, but savory, in a moldy sort of way."

"Shrooms, shrooms," Peg slurped, sucking on a green onion pacifier.

"Mrs. Yin showed me the most beautiful mushrooms she'd found in the woods. Chanterelles, she called them. A gorgeous orange shade, my favorite color. I'll trade for them, plus puffball and stinkbasket mushrooms. Can't wait to experiment!"

Percy could wait. A long time.

"How does mushroom-rye soup sound?" asked Mrs. Veerance. "Could be tasty. Did you know mushrooms have been around for millions of years? They eat decaying material and that's how they exist."

No wonder mushrooms tasted the way they did.

Mr. Veerance said that his brother Linus would still trade with him. "Families support each other," he said. "We can have all the wheat, barley, oats, and rye we want."

(Uncle Linus was the grain farmer. But he was allergic to grain pollen, thus resulting in red watery eyes and a runny nose most of the time. People called him "Sinus Linus." Percy wished he had an uncle with a meat loaf farm, or to some day have one of his own. But that wasn't the family business.)

"And don't forget, all the crickets we want, too," Mrs. Veerance said.

(Percy's Grandpap raised crickets to trade. He housed them in an elaborate facility consisting of furnished apartments, a school house, a playground, feeding troughs, and an auditorium. Grandpap Gence believed that the sound of chirping crickets was vital for the peaceful environment of Yoosa's countryside. He went one step further: he taught the crickets to sing. With lots of practice, his crickets became the best warblers of any insect group in Yoosa. And since only male crickets sing, Grandpap Gence formed the Lady Crickets Orchestra and taught the females to play instruments, miniaturized, of course. The cricket concerts were described by one patron as "an unrivaled musical extravaganza of harmonious ecstasy." Because of the wonderful music they created, the crickets were revered. Men, women, and children came from all over to trade for them.)

"In case you ever get tired of my singing," Mrs. Veerance said, "the crickets can sing for you."

Mr. Veerance looked at his wife longingly. "Vera, you know we'll never tire of your singing. Besides," he said, "I delivered a bushel of summer squash to Telly's farm today and he said his crickets aren't singing up to par because of the lack of sun."

"That's terrible, Vance."

Percy thought so, too. Grandpap Gence's crickets were his pride and joy.

"What is being done about the sun?" asked Mrs. Veerance. "We need it back badly. Have you noticed how manners have faded along with the sun? No one writes thank-you notes anymore!" (Mrs. Veerance thought thank-you notes were the hallmark of a civilized community. She wrote thank-you notes for the thank-you notes she received.)

Even though no one was watching him, Percy stirred the spinach and curried beet casserole around his plate to make it look as if he were eating it.

"I'm serious, Vance. Somebody should be doing something."

Mr. Veerance stuffed more pulp into zucchini tubes. "I am. I'm going to talk to the mayor. The sun's his jurisdiction. He should handle the problem."

"Good idea," Mrs. Veerance said. She surprised Peg with another of her culinary creations, a vegetable pop. She made assorted kinds. Last week, it was cauliflower. This week, Brussels sprouts. Peg gurgled. She sang to Peg:

> *Here's a treat, 'cause you're so sweet,*
> *My little Veggie Peggie, with a head like an eggie,*
> *A sweet little girl with one little curl,*
> *Who goes wee wee wee all the way home.*

Percy gave his mom a weird look. She should trade with the poetry farmer. And the music farmer.

"She's a Piggy Peggie, that little one," Mr. Veerance said. "I got one kid who's skinny and one who's chubby." He clucked his tongue. "Vera, give me a Brussels sprouts pop, will you? I crave them. You should, too, Percy. You know, you are what you eat."

Was that true? Percy wondered who'd ever want to be a Brussels sprout. He hated veggie pops. His mom was the only mom in Yoosa who made them. He wanted his mom to make better-tasting food for better trading, but he had learned a long time ago that his mom had strange tastes. Once he tried to trade a batch of spicy eggplant pops for an adventure book. The book farmer, Mr. Page, laughed so hard he fell down. Percy ran away as fast as he could.

"Next time, Vance," Mrs. Veerance said, "let's have pumpkin toothpaste. Such a beautiful color."

Percy quickly scooped the last of his dinner into a napkin. He carefully lowered it under the table to Dilly. It was Dilly's job to sneak the napkins outside and bury them away from the house. Dilly was a great dog.

"Mom, can I take some veggie pops to Auntie Flora? I think she'd like them." The fewer pops in the house, the better. Percy liked his aunt. He visited her almost every day. She was fun to talk to. She told the best stories and gave good advice. He wanted to tell her the latest about Biff Stuffy, a big lunk of a boy who had recently begun picking on him.

"Don't you want some herbal ice cream for dessert, dear? It's your favorite."

No, it wasn't. Percy never ate that stuff. He'd told his mom many times his favorite flavor was banana, but he couldn't remember the last time they'd had banana ice cream.

"I'll have a bowl of ice cream," Mr. Veerance said.

"Can I go?" asked Percy.

"Go where?" asked Mrs. Veerance.

"To Auntie Flora's."

"I suppose, but don't stay too long."

"Why do you always say that when I'm going over to Auntie's?"

"Do I say that? Hmmm...I don't know," Mrs. Veerance said.

"Is it because the other kids have started calling her 'Flower Freak?'"

Mr. Veerance laughed. "Good one."

"Is that what they call her?" Mrs. Veerance wrinkled her eyebrows. "When we were small, they called my sister 'Airy Fairy.'"

Sometimes his aunt became dreamy, but that didn't bother Percy one bit. And sometimes she made up fanciful sayings she called "Floraisms." Some he understood: "One person's mountain is another person's molehill." And some he didn't: "A buzzy bee is better than a fuzzy flea."

"Mom, why did they call Auntie a fairy?"

"Because she's eccentric."

"Does that mean you don't care what other people think of you?" Percy asked.

"No," Mr. Veerance said. "It means you aren't like other people."

"Is that bad?"

"Yes. Most people only like their own kind."

That didn't sound right, but Percy didn't want to discuss it. He wanted to get going. He signaled Dilly, said good-bye to his parents and little sister, and barged out the back door.

In a mulching pile, Dilly dug a hole and buried the napkin. Percy tossed a handful of veggie pops across the field. "Hey, Dill, where's a hungry gopher when you need one?"

"Ruff!"

Three

Auntie Flora

ERCY'S AUNT WAS A SPIRITED WOMAN, who radiated a style all her own. Her name matched her personality—she loved flowers. In her hair, she wore a garland of sunflower petals which framed her pretty face like the sun's corona. She wore earrings made of pressed rosebuds and corsages on her dresses. She glued dried geranium blossoms to her shoes.

Lately, some Yoosians thought Flora overdid the flowery look—hence the nickname "Flower Freak." Others thought she decorated herself nicely. But all agreed—she smelled really good. Flora was a walking floral display—and air freshener, all in one.

She lived alone in a comfy cottage on a plot of land on the east side of the Veerance farm. Her children were the many varieties of flowers she raised for trading. When Percy was small, he asked her why she grew so many flowers. She told him there was a miracle in every flower. She told him the earth laughed with flowers. And laughter was good, especially for what ailed you. Flora delivered bouquets, nosegays, and wreaths to everyone in Yoosa—whether they wanted to trade with her or not. She left them on people's doorsteps with a note saying she was thinking of them. Since the sun's decline, some people kicked the flowers away. Couldn't be bothered. But those who brought them into their homes told Flora the flowers had brightened their day.

In the distance, Percy spotted his aunt standing in a sea of violas. She petted the flowers as she talked to them. She wore a straw visor woven with daisies. It was the one she called her "sunny hat."

Dilly trotted ahead of Percy into the flower garden. He jumped into Flora's arms, licked her cheek.

"Wonderful to see you, too, Dilly," she said.

Percy trudged into the garden. "Are you going to use your special powder today, Auntie?"

"Nice to see you, too, Percy," Flora said as she mussed Percy's hair. "I most certainly am. A sprinkle a day keeps the doldrums away." She put Dilly down and took a packet from her apron pouch.

Flora invented H.O.P. Powder, named for hope, optimism, and persistence. From flowers that grew the largest, the brightest, and lasted the longest, she took pieces of their roots, pistils, and stamens, combined them together, and ground them up. Even with the loss of sunlight, the flowers dusted with H.O.P. Powder continued to thrive. Flora said it gave them a confident attitude. She sprinkled some powder on the violas. They sprouted up higher, their purple color glowed more vibrantly than before.

"Bobbydazzler!" Percy said.

"Ruff!"

"That's why they're called 'Johnny Jump Ups,'" Flora said.

Percy watched the flowers spring higher. He handed his aunt a Brussels sprouts pop.

She smiled at Percy. "I see my sister, the vegetable cuisine scientist, is at it again!" She laughed cheerfully. "Come inside for cider, and I'll tell you the story about the time when we were little, younger than you are now, and your mom made mung bean pancakes and okra syrup for breakfast."

The interior of Flora's cottage resembled a plant nursery. She liked to have nature around her all the time. Vases of flowers sat on shelves. Pampas grass and bamboo covered the walls. Ferns lined the ceiling. The carpet was a lawn of clover. Flora didn't need to build a greenhouse to cultivate her famed orchids; she lived in one. Nor did she need to sweep her floors; she watered them. In fact, she watered the whole house, including her queen-size bed of roses (de-thorned of course). Before Yoosa's sun problem, whenever Flora misted her house, the sun's rays had shone through the windows, creating an indoor rainbow.

Percy sank into a sofa made from palm fronds. He loved the way the cottage looked and smelled, like a spring day, earthiness, and freshness rolled into one. Dilly enjoyed it, too. Flora let him chew on the furniture. He was especially fond of the dining room table made from dogwood bark.

While Dilly gnawed on a table leg, Flora served Percy poppyseed cookies with ginger-apple cider. She finished her story about the mung bean pancakes:

"Our papa was squeamish about trying your mother's culinary creation. He said he'd prefer to eat a mudcake. So your mom marched right outside, dug up some soil, and made a cake from dirt, water, and grass for icing."

"Did Grandpap Gence eat it?"

"No, he said he'd save it for a special occasion. But the next day I saw him toss it into the compost heap."

"Did you eat it?

"Sure, I didn't want to hurt your mother's feelings."

"How could you?"

"Pure imagination. If you have to eat food you hate, imagine it's something luscious, like strawberry pie. Close your eyes. Pretend you can smell the berries, taste the sweetness, the tartness. Feel the flaky crust swooshing around your mouth. Believe it tastes good, and it does!"

"It would have taken more than imagination to eat my mom's dinner tonight. And the dessert—herbal ice cream. It tastes like eucalyptus leaves! What's wrong with banana or peach ice cream?"

"Your mother tries not to trade with the Xotic Fruit Farm."

"Why?"

"Out of respect for your father. Xavier Xotic courted your mother the same time as your father. They were both intense suitors. But your mother chose Vance, and it worked out wonderfully."

Percy thought, *I could have had a Fruitcake Father instead of a Veggie Pop!*

"While the romance pursuit was progressing, Xavier would send me bushels of his best fruit, hoping I would intercede on his behalf. And that bothered Vance."

"What did you do?"

"Nothing, except I did eat the fruit. It was delicious. But I stay out of people's romances. Love is a complicated thing."

"Why'd Mom pick my dad?"

"She said he made her sing. All Xavier did was work, adding more orchards, hiring more relatives. He tried to impress your mother with the size of his farm. Didn't work. Poor thing never recovered. Some broken hearts never mend. When I trade with Xavier, I try to lift his spirits. Gladiolas are good for that."

Now Percy understood why his mom had him trade with the Xotic Farm when she needed fruit for a recipe, which wasn't often.

"The Xotic Farm keeps getting bigger," Percy said.

"And so many Xotic cousins, I can't remember all their names." Flora counted on her fingers. "There's Xralph, Xroy, Xrex, Xrob. Xrod is the tall one, the thin one is Xray, the loud one, Xrant. And plenty others. I just say, 'Hi, Mr. X,' and leave it at that."

"My dad calls them all 'Xrich.'" Percy finished a cookie, grabbed another one. "I wanted to tell you, Auntie, Biff Stuffy doesn't shove me around anymore, not since I told him jokes like you said I should."

"Wonderful!"

"Whenever I see him coming I say, "Knock, knock."

"Who's there?" Flora said.

"Orange."

"Orange who?"

"Orange you glad you're not me?!" Percy said. "Then I tell him a riddle, like, 'Why'd the chicken lay the egg? Because the pig brought bacon—and it was time for breakfast.'"

"Leave 'em laughing. Good for you, Percy!"

"Maybe I'm starting to fit in with the other farm kids."

"That's not important," Flora said. "Just be yourself. And stand up for yourself." She smiled and raised her eyebrows at Percy for added emphasis—the look she gave him when she wanted him to pay extra attention to what she was saying.

Standing up for yourself wasn't easy. Percy changed the subject. "How's your trading going, Auntie?"

"Not good. As the days get darker, people can't see the beauty of my flowers, so they don't want to trade with me."

"Same with us. No one wants vegetables, so that's all we have to eat. Dad says you are what you eat."

"Your grandpa always told me, 'You are what you think.'"

"Auntie, if Mom liked to sing so much, why didn't Grandpap teach her how to sing in a good voice, like he did for the crickets?"

"He didn't have the heart to tell her she needed voice lessons."

Or cooking lessons either, Percy thought. "Are you going to the town meeting tomorrow night? My dad thinks the mayor might know how to fix the sun problem."

"I'd rather rely on myself than elected officials," Flora said as she pruned her chairs. "As long as I keep plodding along, things go okay."

Percy wrestled with Dilly on the grassy floor. "My mom always says 'Go outside and play.' But inside your house, Auntie, it's like being outside."

"Your mom also wants you home soon," Flora said. She held up a canvas sack. "Here's something for your walk home, a treat from the bird farmer."

Percy jumped up from the floor, looked in the sack. "Turkey jerky! Thanks, Auntie." Dilly wagged his ears. Percy gave him a piece.

"Mr. Fowler is my best customer. Last week he traded an entire barbecued buzzard for one of my marigolds," Flora said.

"Maybe he thought it was made of real gold," Percy said, munching.

"Oh, dear, that would make him a birdbrain," Flora said. She also gave Percy a well-fed orchid. "Here's something for your mother. She works hard."

"I'll have to hide it from Peg. She'll want to eat it."

Four

♩♩♩ Town Meeting

N ORDERS FROM MAYOR OSCAR, Dotty Dash, Yoosa's telegraph farmer, transmitted the message about the town meeting. She used a crisp staccato style, which meant "urgent."

"A town meeting, what's that?"

"Since when do we have town meetings?"

No one knew. There had been no pressing matters of late, or even in recent memory, to warrant a meeting. Occasionally, petty problems cropped up, like Midge Thinley complaining that the barber pole at Bob O'Crew's barber shop farm was too fat. Or Tom Fowler complaining that Bronco Snozhead and his bulky stallion, Stanley, had fallen asleep on a bench in the town square (which was actually a rhomboid) and scared away the pigeons with their combined snoring. But these matters were settled quickly by the mayor. He told people to stop the bickering brattle because he wasn't paid enough to listen to it. Every day was business as usual in Yoosa, until the sun problem.

The citizens of Yoosa, young and old, congregated in the dusty town hall. They crowded on benches, stood on the sidelines, and crammed into the back. Cobwebs draped across the ceiling. Dirt clouded the windows and piled up on the floor. There were no janitor farms in Yoosa. No one wanted the job.

The town hall buzzed with the illustrious citizenry of Yoosa. They gabbed with each other. Duchess Mortimer, the widowed chicken farmer, lamented the demise of three chickens—literally embarrassed to death by their messy chicken coop. Too bad, everyone agreed—especially since her late husband, Egbert had died after she banished him to the chicken coop.

Miss Ursula Fellini, the lingerie farmer, gazed in the direction of Philious Mot, the word farmer. She bragged about her "precocious" (not to mention "precious") cat Pookins, who she said had unwound a ball of silk thread the size of a barrel and then, "incredible as it seems, wound it back again!"

"What's so incredible about that?" someone said.

"Why would you have a ball of thread that big anyway?" said another. "Underwear is little."

"I think it's stupendous," Philious Mot said. "Downright stupefying!"

"Phil's been reading the dictionary again," said Rocky Cardia, the tombstone farmer.

"Oh, yes," sighed Miss Fellini.

Bard Leary, the poetry farmer, crept inside the hall and sat next to Phil Mot. He was late for the meeting because he'd been writing by the lake all afternoon and with little sunlight, lost track of time. (Mr. Leary spent most of his time at the lakes, Dreary and Cheery, because he rhymed with them.)

"How's the sonnet writing?" Phil asked.

"Grueling," Bard said. "What's a word that rhymes with vivacious?"

"Bodacious, loquacious," Phil replied.

"Pugnacious," Rocky Cardia said.

"Ostentatious," Duchess Mortimer said.

"So pretentious," cracked Midge Thinley, the cracker farmer, a waif of a woman.

"I don't like big words," said Frannie Tubula, the hair curler farmer and a deluxe-sized woman. "But I do like big hair and big meals."

"Now, now, Cupcake," said Icabod Tubula, Frannie's husband, the bobby pin and matchstick farmer who resembled his products.

"You brought me a cupcake?!" Mrs. Tubula kissed her husband's sunken cheek. "You sweet thing, you know I love sweets and—"

And on and on, Yoosians chattered while waiting for the meeting to begin. The topic of conversation turned to the fading sun.

"Have you noticed there's no more afternoon sun?" said Needle-Nose Nelson, the pencil farmer.

"How could we not?" said Cyril Klops, the eyeglasses farmer. "We're not blind!"

"It's so chilly during the day, especially when you're sitting on a pile of bricks," said Nicky Brickhauser, the brick farmer's wife.

"I can't tell what time it is anymore. How am I supposed to know when to eat?"

"Or sleep?"

"It's ruining my health," said Mr. Borden, the hatchet farmer, who hacked away in the corner with a bad cough.

"Mine, too," sniffed Mrs. Hydrans, her nose congested.

"I caught a chest cold," said Wellington Wellington Stuffy, the stuffed shirt farmer. He wheezed, his chest rattling like a bucket full of rocks. His wife, Zoe Stuffy, the throw rug farmer, put her arm around him.

"The sun problem is ruining my livelihood."

bowls won't harden."

"Mine, too," said Mu Nu Abu, the boot farmer. "My leather won't tan."

"Mine, too," said Linus Veerance. "My grains are molding."

"Mine, too," said Jericoe Jumpin' Jupiter ("Triple Jay," as he liked to be called), the ball, stick, and hoop farmer. "Who can play ball in the dark?"

"Mine, too," said Viv Id, the sequin farmer. "No one's in the mood to dress up anymore." Viv sewed sequins on all her clothes and on her kids' clothes, too. But her husband, Tim, refused to wear them.

"Mine, too," said Mr. Sushiyama. "The fish are too depressed to eat, so I can't catch them. We're hungry," he said sadly, looking at his three daughters: Polly, Holly, and Golly (who had been a surprise).

"What are we going to do?" said Pat, the pancake farmer. Or was it Pat, the cappuccino farmer? No one could tell them apart. They played patty-cake with the Id kids, Goldie and Glossy.

"I say stay warm," said Spotty Kismet, the blanket and quilt farmer, who lounged on the bench with his wife Flooie, the pillow farmer. (They were newlyweds and popular farmers, as Yoosians were early-to-bed, early-to-rise kinds of folks.)

In the back row of the hall sat Kay Oss, the junk farmer, surrounded by a mound of unidentifiable stuff. She considered her stuff valuable; some called it rubbish. (Aunt Flora had told Percy that one person's trash was another person's treasure, and vice-versa.)

"Life is filled with disorder," said Kay. "Get used to it."

"What do you care?" said Rocky Cardia, the tombstone farmer. "Your business is harum-scarum. Mine is set in stone."

"I beg your pardon!" Kay stood, hands on her hips. "My business is willy-nilly, thank you very much!"

"Topsy-turvy," Phil Mot said.

"Topsy-turvy," Phil Mot said.

The volume of complaining increased. So did the negative tone. The town hall sounded like a swarm of hornets nesting in a beehive where they hadn't been invited.

Percy tuned out the buzz. He sat in the second row with his family. Across the room he spotted Buckminster Dent, the dental floss farmer. He waved but did not smile. Mr. Dent always stared at Percy's teeth. (He stared at everyone's teeth.) Mr. Dent had brought along his pet moose, Bruce. He said that moose teeth were the best to practice flossing on. Mona's teeth were second best. Percy had dragged Mona to the Dent Farm for flossing lessons, which was how Percy and Mr. Dent became friends.

Percy had asked him why he had a dental floss farm.

"Two reasons, Percy," Mr. Dent said. "Vanity and fear. Any business that appeals to those two traits will be prosperous. People want to look good—vanity, and they're afraid of losing their teeth—fear. You could say as far as business goes, I hit the molar on the head!"

Percy had asked Auntie Flora what her flower business appealed to. She said, "A sense of aesthetics." Whatever that meant didn't sound prosperous to Percy. He asked his dad what their vegetable farm appealed to. Mr. Veerance said, "Quit asking so many questions and eat your rutabaga!"

Dilly and Bruce the Moose had also become friends. Bruce gave Dilly rides on his back. Dilly steered Bruce by turning his antlers from side to side. Now, back in the town hall, Percy knew Dilly wanted to wave his ear at Bruce, but Percy told Dilly to lay low.

The entire front row was occupied by the ample Clumpie family, cottage cheese farmers. Clirving and his wife Clara had six strapping sons: Cladam, Clabraham, Claaron, Clarthur, Clandrew, and Spike. The boys' shoulders formed a massive wall across the bench. The

Clumpies had to farm cottage cheese because Clumpie cow milk came out sour—undrinkable. Everyone in Yoosa knew why Clumpie milk was unpleasant—Clumpie cows were not happy. They were over-worked, stressed out. They were not allowed to relax or take coffee breaks. Occasionally, the cows went on strike. But those quickly ended when the cows were turned into leather goods. Sometimes, the cows escaped to the Happy Clown Farm and joined the circus. (The cow act consisted of jumping through hoops of fire, which apparently was con-sidered a better job than working for the Clumpies.)

Percy and his family sat behind the Clumpies. His dad sat as tall as he could, his head bobbing from side to side to see around the block-ade. Uncle Linus sat to the left of him. He shucked wheat stalks and blew his nose. His mom sat next to Percy. She held Peg, stroking the baby's one tuft of hair. Percy watched in discomfort when Cladam and Clabraham stretched their arms, squishing their mother, Clara, between them. Vera and Clara were trading partners. Both liked to pre-pare cheesy vegetable pies for their families. The Clumpie Brothers never ate vegetables. Percy had no choice.

Clara turned to chat with Vera. "Your Peg is *sooo* adorable. I'll trade you a couple of my boys for Peg."

"No thanks," Vera said.

"Three boys?" Mrs. Clumpie asked.

"No trade."

Percy looked relieved, but wondered if his mom would ever trade *him* for a Clumpie. (Clumpies would blend in better with the furniture, especially the plank table.)

Percy knew the Clumpie Brothers wouldn't turn around to speak to him. They never acknowledged his presence; they thought he was too puny to bother with. So he continued to slouch on the bench—first, because he felt so small compared to the Clumpie Brothers—and second, because he didn't want to be seen by Vic Brickhauser and the Malatete Twins, farm kids who picked on him (for being a pea picker). He knew they were lurking somewhere in the hall, but he didn't know where. Luckily, Dilly hunkered beneath the bench and kept a lookout for him. Dilly was a great dog. Percy dreaded a confrontation with Vic and the Malatetes, especially in front of his dad. He had not thought of any new jokes. He needed to do that soon. *Knock knock....*

Someone tapped Percy on his shoulder.

"Who's there?" Percy looked up. It was Mr. Fowler.

"Is your aunt here?" he asked.

Percy shook his head.

"I wanted to show her my auk."

Mayor Oscar pounded with his gavel on a podium at the front of the hall. "Attention, everyone! Let the meeting begin."

Chattering continued. Yoosians were not used to coming to attention.

"I made that gavel," said Udell Woodruff, the woodworking and wooden furniture farmer. Mr. Woodruff had a side-line business: artificial wooden limbs. Sooner or later, he measured everyone in Yoosa and made an exact replica of his or her right leg and arm. He labeled and stored them on wooden racks in his barn. To date, no one in Yoosa had lost a limb, but Udell was ready if anyone did.

(When Percy asked Farmer Woodruff what would happen, for instance in a plowing accident, if his left leg got chopped off, Mr. Woodruff had replied, "That would be tough luck, gimpy.")

The mayor pounded again. He narrowed his eyes and looked stern. His sausage-shaped nose turned red. His head bounced up and down as he rapped. His varnished hair didn't budge. It was so stiff, it wouldn't move if you lifted him up by his heels and shook him. "QUIIII—ET!"

he shouted. His head looked ready to implode. (Nothing could explode through that shield of hair.)

The chatter faded.

"Thank you. You all know why you're here. Twenty score and four years ago, our Yoosian forefathers brought forth upon this land a spiffy community conceived of farms and dedicated to—"

"Get to the point," someone yelled.

"This speech could be famous some day," the mayor said.

"We don't care!"

"All right. Let me continue," said the mayor. "I've made promises. Some I've kept, and some I had no intentions of... well... that's not important. What is important, however, my intelligent loyal constituents, is that I have good news which shall be beneficial to you, especially you of voting age, and—"

"Nip it in the bud, Mayor!"

"We didn't elect you to talk our ears off," said Euterpe Hardwicke, the soap farmer.

"I need my ears," said Euterpe's husband, Chester, the flute farmer.

"So do I," said Maestro Muzacky, the music farmer.

The mayor looked dejected. "It's not like we have these meetings all the time."

"Stick a sock in your piehole, Mayor!" Rocky Cardia said.

"Desist with the logorrhea," Philious Mot said.

"My, aren't we a cranky bunch." The mayor looked defeated. "Very well," he said. "Here's the short version: I have ascertained that the sun problem is due to the fact that the rope holding the sun in place at the peak of Amethyst Mountain is coming loose, causing the sun to drift away. Now, all we need is someone to hike up the mountain, pull the sun back in, and secure the rope. Simple enough. Then Yoosa goes back to normal. Any volunteers?"

The room became as still as the Yoosa cemetery at midnight (on the nights when Rocky Cardia wasn't out and about admiring his handiwork, in which case gleeful chortling could be heard).

The mayor looked around the hall. "Volunteers?" he said again.

Mr. Snozhead pretended to sleep.

No-Lips Barney shook his head so hard that his three teeth clattered. The flies flitting around his head stopped midair.

Most people looked down. All remained silent. Percy's dad stared at the ceiling. His mom looked like a statue.

"Anyone?"

"We're too busy," said a voice from the back.

"Doing what?" asked the mayor.

All at once, people called out:

"Snoring."   "Stuffing."
"Weaving."   "Flossing."
"Barbering."   "Reading."
"Shearing."   "Telegraphing."

"Pruning, harvesting, canning, preserving, juicing, jamming, and jellying."

Vance Veerance looked over his shoulder, spied Xavier Xotic. "Egads!" he said under his breath.

"Eating," Mrs. Tubula said.

"Dieting," Mrs. Thinley said.

"Creating," Bard Leary said.

"Playing," Triple Jay said.

"Worrying!"

"You got that right!"

The mayor scratched his helmet head. "Those aren't very good reasons," he said. "Each day gets shorter. Sunrises appear later. Sunsets fade quicker. Isn't anyone willing to keep Yoosa from turning into a dark and desolate place forever?"

Breathing seemed to stop. Needle-Nose Nelson dropped a pencil on the floor. Everyone heard it.

Percy looked around. Surely someone would volunteer. It was so important. But he could tell by their expressions, no one was going anywhere near the mountain.

The mayor asked, "How about you, Clirving? I see you sitting there with your big boys. Certainly one of you can go?"

"Sorry, Mayor. This is clotting season. Very critical time for us. Can't leave clots unattended."

"It's not just the time factor, Oscar," said Turner Page, the book farmer. "You're asking someone to take a big risk. I've read many books that warn about the treacherous terrain on Amethyst Mountain. A trek up the mountain would be a dangerous undertaking."

"Perilous, pernicious, perishable," Philious Mot said.

"No one's ever made it to the peak that I know about," Dick Brickhauser said.

"I got enuff trubble," said Bronco Snozhead, the horse trader. "I don't go lookin' for it."

"I don't either," Vance Veerance said.

"I heard there are trolls up there," Yardley Ewing said.

"I heard there are monsters up there," Mo'poke Malatete said.

"I heard evil spirits roam freely where the deer and antelope used to play," Leo Hohokam said.

"And don't forget Grizzman!" Old Man Pops said. The old folks gasped. Granny Prunella fainted.

"Remember Farmer Bell? He went up there and never came back!"

"Grizzman probably got him."

"Who's Grizzman?" Percy whispered to his mom. She looked blank.

"Do you understand the consequences for us?" the mayor said. "For all of Yoosa, if no one volunteers?"

No one responded.

"For the last time, I need a volunteer!" THWANK! Mayor Oscar slammed the gavel.

"All systems are unstable. Get used to it," Kay Oss said.

"No one is dumb enough to volunteer."

"Very well," the mayor said. "I'll give you time to think about the situation and what you personally can do. We'll meet again. But don't forget, the sun problem is *not* someone else's problem—it's all of ours. And it's *not* just a matter of convenience, it's a matter of life and death."

Five

Flora's Advice

THE NEXT MORNING THE SUN APPEARED hours later than usual for a summer day. And unlike a summer day, the cold air nipped Percy's bare feet while he sat at the breakfast plank. He stirred his spoon around a bowl of garbanzo bean porridge. He wished it would evaporate. He thought of dipping his feet in the bowl—squishing his toes in the steamy goop to warm them—but if his dad saw, he would get in trouble. Imagining his toes mashed in the porridge made it even harder to eat. He carefully dumped a spoonful into a napkin on his lap, folded it in half, added another spoonful, and....

"Did you hear me, Percy?" asked Mr. Veerance.

"What, Dad?"

"Do you want to swat flies with me after work?"

"Can't," Percy said, "I'm busy." He stuffed the napkin in his overalls pocket. "Got to get going." He gave the rest of his porridge to Peg. She squealed, dug her hands in the bowl. Percy left through the back door with Dilly at his side. He heard his mom ask who slammed the door.

❀ ❀ ❀

In the radish field, Percy used a different method of harvesting this morning—quick and careless. No time to measure and inspect. He moved quickly through the rows, his arms rotating like a windmill. He pulled and tossed the radishes in record speed. Dilly loped behind him, batting the radishes into piles as fast as Percy picked them. Row after row.

Percy felt the sweat roll down his back. After the twenty-fourth and last row, he stopped and rubbed his back. His legs hurt from crouching so long; his arms ached from all the tossing. One more bag to go. Percy held open a burlap sack. Dilly scooted radishes into it with his snout. "Good job, boy! Time for a break. Are you as pooped as me?"

"Ruff!"

Percy spread out on the ground and rested. The earth was soft and comforting. He tucked his arms behind his head. Dilly plopped on Percy's stomach. Percy stared at the sun. It looked like a burned-out lump of orange-colored coal. What would happen to their farm if the sun drifted away completely? With no sunlight at all, there'd be no vegetables to eat. That would be good. But then there'd be nothing to trade with. And that would be bad! Hadn't anyone heard what Mayor Oscar said? It was "a matter of life and death." What was really happening on top of the mountain? Wasn't anybody the least bit curious? And who was Grizzman? Percy closed his eyes and tried to imagine a monster mountain-man. But he couldn't. He was glad.

"Come on, Dill. We need to see Auntie. I promised we'd help her today."

Percy was eager to visit his aunt and hear her opinion about the town meeting. Plus, she had said that after they made flower arrangements, she had a surprise for them both. This usually meant a new book for him and a chew toy for Dilly—their favorite things, next to good food.

They found Flora in a bed of irises. She was working hard, snipping stalks and trimming leaves. She wore her snapdragon hat. Percy knew this meant his aunt was in a serious gardening mood. She delegated the workload for making bouquets: Dilly rolled out spools of purple ribbon; Percy cut it into strips. Flora arranged the flowers, and Percy held the bunches together as she tied bows around them. Dilly held the bouquets by the ribbon and carried them to a cart. They made a great team. Flora exclaimed throughout the process, "Wonderful! Wonderful!"

As they worked, Percy told his aunt what had happened at the town hall meeting.

"I'm glad I didn't go," Flora said. "Sounds like not much was accomplished." She concentrated on sorting flowers. "By the way, was Bard there?"

"He came late. All he said was 'Hey, nonny nonny.'"

"I'm surprised. Not exactly a poetic setting."

"Grandpap couldn't go. One of his crickets caught a bug, so he had to stay home."

"I went to Buena Hayseed's farm last night. We made straw dolls for her to trade. I snagged some extra straw for Mona."

Percy hoped a straw doll wasn't his surprise. That would be awful. Then he'd have to write a thank-you note, like when Uncle Linus gave him a dozen wool handkerchiefs for his ninth birthday and he didn't know what to do with them. His mother kept after him to write the note. It took Percy two months to think up what to say.

"Dear Uncle Linus," he had written, "thank you for the hankies. They come in handy. I use them all the time. One time I used one to tie around Dilly's head when he had an earache. Thanks for remembering my birthday. Your favorite nephew (ha ha), Percy." (Linus only had one nephew.)

All true in the note. But Percy hadn't used the handkerchiefs to blow his nose. They'd smelled funny and were scratchy. Instead, he'd used them to stuff food into when his mom's vegetable experiments had gone wrong. Dilly had buried the whole mess in a field.

"How did the meeting end?" asked Flora.

"Mayor Oscar asked for a volunteer. Everyone wants the sun back but no one wants to volunteer."

"You won't possess what you're unwilling to pursue," Flora said.

Another Floraism. This one made sense. (Most didn't, like "A fly on the wall is the wisest of all." Percy had asked his mom why his aunt made up sayings. She said Flora had been born under a philosopher's stone—which didn't make much sense either.)

Flora said she knew the story of the origin of the sun's being tethered to Amethyst Mountain. Percy begged to hear it. She agreed, as long as they kept working.

Any task was worth a good story!

Flora began:

> Long ago, when Yoosa was covered with primeval vegetation and metamorphic rock, and evolving species crawled from tide pools, the elements ran wild. Rain, hail, wind, fog, snow, thunder, drizzle, lightning, and sunshine all came and went freely.
>
> Ancient Yoosians lived in caves. To eat, they hunted. To hunt, they planned ahead. They needed seasons, a time to

perform every activity. But that was not to be. Hunting became too difficult because the elements were too difficult to predict. To survive, Yoosians of yore decided to grow crops. Success in this endeavor required three ingredients: soil, water, and sunlight. Fertile land was plentiful. A steady source of water was obtained from the cheery pond and dreary lake.

But the sun was another matter entirely. It was not reliable. It bobbed about the sky like a loose kite, floated by as it pleased, but never on a set schedule. Sometimes the sun hung around all day, other days not at all. The sun needed to be cyclical. It needed to be harnessed. But how?

Yoosians went to the mightiest hunter they knew for help, a young man named Rasco, who was said to be as strong as a dozen men. Rasco knew what to do. He asked his sister, Lasco, the smartest girl in Yoosa. She had an idea. She went to Zeal Crater—where long before a comet had fallen—and retrieved the silver strands from the comet's tail. She braided them together and formed a rope long enough to reach far into the heavens.

Lasco, Rasco, and the whole community hiked to the summit of Amethyst Mountain and waited for the sun to drift by. When it did, Rasco twirled the silver rope in a huge circle, flung it into the sky, and lassoed the sun.

Twenty men held the sun in place while Rasco yanked a fifty-foot redwood tree from the ground. He ripped off all the branches. With a huge knife, he whittled the tree into a gigantic javelin with a spiral end. Around the other end, he tied the rope that held the sun. With all his might, he plunged the javelin into the earth. The force was so great that the ground trembled as the spear revolved like a spinning corkscrew, carving a tunnel to the center of the earth. Lasco told her brother to wrap the rope around a boulder, then roll the boulder on top of the tunnel to seal it and forever anchor the sun above Yoosa. As Rasco rolled, everyone cheered. A celebration lasted three days and three nights.

"And that's how the sun was captured and became the crown jewel of Amethyst Mountain," Flora said.

"What a great story, Auntie," Percy said. "I'd like to go to the top of the mountain and check it out, but I'm too afraid."

"Sometimes fear can motivate you."

"Mr. Dent says fear makes people want dental floss. When I get scared, my hair sticks up."

"We all get scared from time to time. And we have two choices: face the fear or run away."

"Facing it is better, right?"

Flora smiled and raised her eyebrows.

Percy knew that the raised eyebrows meant that his aunt wanted what she'd said to sink in.

They finished making bouquets, loaded up the cart, and headed back to Flora's cottage.

"Percy, you have the ability to climb the mountain," Flora said. "And you're smart enough to figure out how to fix the sun."

"Ruff!"

"I know you could do it."

"Auntie, I'm not brave enough."

"You don't have to be brave, you just have to plod."

"What's that?"

"One foot forward, then another. That's all it takes."

"One foot after the other? I don't get it."

"It's persistence. Steady plodding brings prosperity. Think about it. You conquer by continuing."

Percy didn't want to think about it. Too much philosophy. His aunt's eyebrows were probably stuck in the up position.

Inside Flora's cottage, Percy jumped on a pile of leaves on the grass carpet. "At last night's meeting, Old Man Pops said there's a someone named Grizzman who lives on the mountain. Have you heard of him?"

"When I was little," Flora said, "a teacher told me a tale about a Grizzman."

"Tell me the story," Percy said.

"Another story?"

Percy pleaded with his face.

"It's a long one," Flora said. "Doesn't your mom want you home?"

"She doesn't know where I am. Please, Auntie?"

Flora switched to her daffodil hat. Percy knew what that meant: his aunt said her "daffy hat" made her feel whimsical. Perfect for story-telling. She began the tale....

Six

The Legend of Barry Grizzman

ONCE UPON A TIME IN YOOSA LIVED widget farmers named Ma and Pa Grizzman. They had one child, a boy named Barry. He was born with a strange affliction: *protrudinous lumpiiosis.* Lumps grew underneath his skin, distorting his body and face. Yoosians had never seen this ailment before. Some stared at baby Barry. Others couldn't bear to look at him. Most pitied him.

Ma and Pa Grizzman hoped their son would outgrow his condition, but he never did. In fact, as Barry grew, so did the number and size of his lumps. Ma Grizzman tried to rub them away, but all she succeeded in doing was rubbing Barry's skin raw. She gave up and never touched him again. The lumps bothered Pa Grizzman so much that he eventually refused to look at his son. Embarrassed by Barry, the Grizzmans isolated themselves on their farm. They stopped trading with other farmers.

When Barry was ten years old, his mother became pregnant. Ma Grizzman feared her newborn would turn out like Barry. Pa Grizzman said Barry was a curse and their new baby should not be exposed to him. Secretly, they sold their farm to the Glazersmiths, put a sack of solid gold widgets on Barry's pillow, and moved away in the middle of the night. When Barry woke the next morning, the new owners kicked him out. They turned the property into a knick-knack farm, which is why there are no more widgets in Yoosa.

Barry was homeless—nowhere to go, no place to live, no friends or relatives to take him in. All alone, he did the best he could. He hid in the walnut orchard and kept to himself. People said it made him nutty.

"The walnuts?" Percy asked.

"No, the isolation," Flora said.

"How did he survive?"

He scavenged food at night when Yoosians were asleep. He built a fort in the tallest tree where no one else could climb. He lived there for many years.

When Barry was a teenager, a girl his age began playing under the walnut tree where he lived. Her hair was brown with golden streaks, tied with a blue ribbon into a bun. Each day the girl and her bride doll had tea parties with cream cakes. Barry sat quietly in the branches, watching. Some days he thought about scaring her away and snatching the cakes. But that was too mean. One day the girl brought chocolate cream cakes decorated with chocolate sprinkles. They smelled delicious. Barry hadn't tasted chocolate in years. He was starving for something sweet—for any food at all! He moved toward the end of a branch and leaned down to get a better whiff. But he leaned too far and fell off, landing on his head with a horrible crash! Startled, the girl jumped up. She knew Barry was hurt, but she didn't know what to do.

"What *did* she do?" Percy asked.

"She sat by him, gently stroking his face as the afternoon light faded."

When Barry opened his eyes, the first thing he saw was the girl's smiling face and the radiance from the sunset lighting her head. "Where am I?" he said.

"On the ground. You got knocked out when you fell from the tree."

"Are you a spirit?"

She laughed. "No, I'm a real girl. You're not dead, if that's what you're thinking."

"But no one in Yoosa has ever been nice to me."

"Maybe they don't know you. I've never seen you before. What's your name?"

"Barry."

"You seem fine now, Barry. It's late and I have to go home. I live at the archery farm, a long walk from here." The girl picked up her doll and her tea set. She gave Barry the last cream cake. "Take it. You've had a rough day." She glided away through the walnut orchard.

"Thanks!" Barry stuffed the whole cake into his mouth and licked the plate clean. "Wait!" he called after the girl. "What's your name?"

Drifting through a soft breeze he heard a melodic sound: "Angela."

That night Barry couldn't sleep, couldn't stop thinking about Angela. He wanted to see her again. But she wouldn't want to see him, not with his hideous lumpy body. His own parents couldn't stand looking at him. He would scare her away, too. What could he do? He remembered his mother often spoke about a "miracle man" who lived on Amethyst Mountain. Maybe this man could work a miracle on him and make his lumps disappear. Barry set out to find him.

Halfway up the mountain, Barry found a cabin. A sign posted on the door read: "P.T. Foolem—Miracle Practitioner. All paying customers welcome." Full of hope, Barry pounded on the door.

P.T. told Barry, "I can perform the miraculous or the mundane, depending on which you can afford."

"Can you make my lumps go away?" asked Barry.

"Easy as pie, but more expensive. How much ya got, kid?"

Barry said not much, as he was saving the sack of gold widgets to start a farm in Yoosa when he got older.

"What kind of farm?" P.T. asked.

"Nuts."

"You are nuts. Your body is downright hideous. You have a chance to be good lookin'. Make up your mind, kid. What'll it be? Beauty or peanuts?"

Barry pondered for only a second. Without lumps, he could see Angela again. That was the most important thing. "Get rid of the lumps, sir," Barry said, as he handed over the bag of widgets.

In the front yard of the cabin, P.T. told Barry to sit in the magic circle and close his eyes. While P.T. danced a jig, he waved a baton over Barry's head. He chanted mysterious mumbo jumbo.

Barry snuck a glimpse. P.T. looked silly hopping around.

"And now, the crucial part," P.T. said. "Open your eyes!" He held an ornate crystal decanter pulsating with swirls of blue and purple. "Jest Juice," he cried. "Drink!"

Barry drank. The substance tasted like liquid lightning—crackling and silvery. It produced an immediate reaction. His skin tingled. He felt cold, then hot, then itchy, then as if explosives were bursting inside him. Before his eyes he saw flashes of blue and purple. He curled up on the ground until the internal explosions stopped.

"Ta da! Gorgeous! You're finished, kid. Have a look." P.T. held up a mirror.

Barry looked at his reflection and shrieked in revulsion. His face and body were covered with long spiky hairs like a prickly pear cactus. "I'm finished, all right! I'm worse than before! Now I'm 'Scary Hairy Barry the Cactus Face!'" Barry doubled over and wailed; his cry echoed all the way down Amethyst Mountain.

"Hey, kid, the lumps are gone, ain't they?" P.T. said. "That's what you paid for. Now go on, get outta here! I'm gonna go spend the gold on myself."

"The lumps aren't gone, you fake! They're just covered up!"

"They don't call me a larcenous lardy-dardy for nuthin'."

Barry fumed, burning inside with rage. He yanked at the hair on his face, but it wouldn't budge. He gyrated himself into a tizzy.

P.T. looked frightened.

"Aaahhh!" Barry screamed so hard that a gale of wind blasted from his mouth. The gale lifted P.T.'s cabin from its foundation and into the air. All of P.T.'s belongings fell out through the windows. The cabin crashed back to the ground with a tumultuous thud. Barry was amazed that he could blow so hard. He blew again, even harder this time. The cabin flew so high into the sky it disappeared from sight. Barry stomped off, hiding his face in his hands. His journey ended at the crest of the mountain where the cabin had landed. Barry appropriated it for himself, and that's where he's lived ever since.

"Is that the end?" asked Percy.

"No."

"Good! Keep going."

"Ruff!"

Near his cabin one day, Barry found a baby wolf, practically dead and with a broken leg, abandoned by its pack. Barry named him Grolf and nursed him back to health. He became Barry's first and only friend. Each night, Grolf fell asleep on the mound of hair on Barry's chest, listening to the same story about a beautiful girl with chocolate cream cakes.

Years passed and still Barry could not forget Angela. He desired to see her so much. And for Grolf to see her, too. But what would be his excuse to go to her home? Certainly not that his heart ached for her. There had to be a practical reason for his visit. He thought and thought. Of course! He'd return her plate—the one she had handed him years ago. But next to Grolf, the plate had become his prized possession. He thought and thought again. He decided people and pets were more important than things.

Barry and Grolf embarked on an expedition down the mountainside. Barry found the archery farm and hoped Angela still lived there. He felt anxious, yet bold at the same time. He strode up onto the porch. On the front door was a stained glass apple with an arrow through it.

Barry knocked on the door, held his breath. The door opened. Angela stared. Barry exhaled. He held out the plate.

Angela stepped onto the porch and looked at it, then at the face before her. "Barry?" she asked. He nodded. Angela smiled. She touched Barry's hairy cheek. "I wondered if I would ever see you again. Oh, what a cute wolf." She scratched Grolf's head.

From inside the house came a tough voice: "Who's at the door, Angela?"

"It's Barry, father," she said. "My friend."

"I don't know anyone named Barry." Angela's father marched to the door. Taking one look at Barry, he hollered, "Blazing Beelzebub! A beast! Quick, Angela, into the house!" He wrenched her back inside. "Don't worry, I'll get my bow and arrows... I'll kill the ogre...."

Angela cried, "Run, Barry, run!"

Every spiky hair on Barry's body sprung up. He tucked the plate under his arm and high-tailed it across the farm. Grolf galloped by his side so fast that his paws barely touched the ground. A barrage of arrows zinged past them. Just as they came to the woods, Barry heard a yelp. He looked down. An arrow gored Grolf in the back. Barry picked him up and screamed so hard at Angela's father that he blew him off the porch and into the house.

Barry bounded as fast as he could up the mountain to his cabin. Sobbing, he held Grolf all night long. But at daybreak, Grolf died in Barry's arms.

Dilly buried his head in a pile of leaves and whimpered. Percy wiped away a tear. His cowlick drooped. "That's so sad, Auntie. Is that the end of the story?"

"One more part."

Seven

Percy Volunteers

ACCORDING TO LEGEND, Barry metamorphosed into Grizzman the Madman, revenge seeker. Whenever anything bad happened in Yoosa, such as a farm house burning down or a storm demolishing an apple grove, people would mutter, "Curse of Grizzman." Over the years, Grizzman sightings diminished. So did the legacy of terror. People began to forget about him. Newer generations had never heard of him. But from time to time, the older folks reminisced and wondered: if Grizzman were still alive, what was he going to do next?

Percy and Dilly ambled home from Flora's cottage, following the sandy path around the flower beds and vegetable fields. They took the long way, so Percy could start reading the book his aunt had given him. (No straw doll!) He tried to read but couldn't concentrate; he kept thinking about Grizzman and his unhappy life. Maybe he still lived on the mountain. If so, he'd have to be very old, maybe too old to be alive. What did he look like? Was he as scary as everyone said? Was he really a madman? (Percy hoped not.) Why wasn't anyone else curious to know what had happened to him?

Percy shivered. The day felt like winter and looked just as bleak without the sun. What would his family do when the real winter came? How would they stay warm? Percy's dad had said he couldn't trade for wood. And they needed wood to burn for heat. Dilly would suffer the most during a freezing winter. He didn't have fur to protect his body. Unless the sun returned, Percy would have to get Dilly warm clothes—maybe a wool coat or a sweater and knit cap. Would other farmers trade vegetables for them? Would there be any vegetables left by then? Percy had hoped when winter came he could trade for Scoot Boots with Mu Nu Abu, the boot farmer. Scoot Boots had corrugated soles, good for traction in inclement weather. All the kids had them, except Percy and the Id kids, who wore sequined sneakers.

He thought about what Auntie Flora had said about plodding. How do you do it? One foot forward in front of the other—too easy. How could that work? There must be more to it. Grizzman, winter weather, clothes for Dilly, plodding—too many things for his brain to ponder at one time. Percy rubbed his forehead.

Something rustled in the oleander hedges on the other side of the path. Percy stopped to listen. He heard voices whispering. Then he heard loud and clear: "Hey, Percy, you pea picker!" and lots of laughing. Just what he didn't need: the Malatete Twins!

"You weed picker!" Mo'poke Malatete said. She threw a handful of stones.

"Oww!" The cowlick on Percy's head jumped up.

"Toe jam picker!"

"Scab picker!"

"Nose picker!"

Dilly growled.

For a moment, Percy flashed on what his aunt had said about fear—facing up to it or running away. What should he do? Stay or run? Stay or run? He ran. Dilly was right behind him. When another rock hit Percy in the back, he stopped. "Hold it, Dill. Let's not run. I have an idea. Watch me." Percy turned back toward the oleander hedges. He took one deliberate step forward, followed by another. Again and again. Dilly imitated him.

The Malatete Twins crawled from the hedges, a confused look contorted their mini-thug faces. "Whatcha doin', pea-picker?" Mo'reen yelled.

Percy paid no attention. He plodded. He was a natural!

Mo'poke yelled, "Hey, Percy, if I pound you into the dirt, who picks *you* out of the ground?"

The twins hooted. Percy kept plodding. The twins scratched their boxy heads. "Hey, Percy, what kind of pea-pickin' trick is this?"

"No, trick," Percy said. "I'm plodding."

"What for?"

"It's fun."

Mo'reen's face squinched up. "I know fun, and *that's* no fun."

Mo'poke grunted. He grabbed Mo'reen's pigtail and yanked on it. She stabbed him with a stick. He socked her in the nose. She poked him in the ear and said, "Now, that's fun!" They schlepped away, throwing rocks at each other.

"Bobbydazzler!" said Percy. "I like this plodding stuff."
"Ruff!"

✵ ✵ ✵

As he plodded home, Percy's spirits soared. He couldn't wait to tell his dad about plodding. He found him behind the house at the compost heap. Peg was playing in the soggy dirt.

"Hey, Peggie," Percy said, "somebody needs a real bath, not a mud bath."

"Bub ba, bub ba."

Mr. Veerance furiously shoveled smelly soil into burlap sacks. Percy held his nose. The odor from cooking vegetables was bad enough, but rotting vegetables was the worst smell on earth. Without looking up, Mr. Veerance said, "Percy, quit holding your nose and help me. Tie up the sacks."

"Sure, Dad. Can I show you something first?"

"No!"

"It's something Auntie Flora—"

"Not now!" Mr. Veerance threw down his shovel and tossed a sack of soil at Percy's feet. "Spread this over the cauliflower field. We're losing the crops without the sun."

"When I'm finished, can I show you?" Percy asked.

"I don't have time for games. And take Peg back to the house. I don't have time to watch her. Then start on the artichoke fields."

✵ ✵ ✵

As the days darkened, Yoosians went about their business more slowly than usual, since they were tired from so much worrying. Their moods worsened in proportion to the sun's decline. People became more crabby, which turned out to be a contagious condition, as a large portion of Yoosians turned into sourpusses.

A senior citizens club was formed by Old Man Pops. They called themselves the Pettifog Fogies. Membership included Quilda Yin, the mushroom farmer; Udell Woodruff, the woodworking farmer; Cyril Klops, the eyeglasses farmer; Ignatia Glazersmith, the knick-knack farmer (and collectible collector extraordinaire—over two thousand ceramic frogs and counting); and Saffron Pepperaji, the spunky herb and spice farmer whom the other members relied on to add pizzazz to their group.

Each afternoon the Fogies reclined on one of Udell's handmade park benches, measuring the duration of sunlight. They calculated that it lasted less than five hours per day. They devised a classification system to describe the sky's colors, such as slate gray, pile of ashes gray, dead-fish gray, and mushroom juice gray. They posted the data on the rhomboidal town square bulletin board. As sunlight decreased, ill-mannered descriptions by the Fogies increased. For instance, they described the sky as Midge Thinley's scrawny pet bird gray or Euterpe Hardwicke's dirty sheets gray.

Other off-color color descriptions included: Pookins the spoiled cat gray, Clirving Clumpie's bad batch of cottage cheese gray, Sinus Linus snot rag gray, Mayor Oscar's bad-fitting toupee gray, Bronco Snozhead's even worse-fitting dentures gray, and Rocky Cardia's heart turned-to-stone gray.

(Philious Mot called the group's comments insensate, insolent, and insulting.)

The sun problem was responsible for tragedies in Yoosa. While stacking bricks in the dark, a pile fell on Mr. and Mrs. Brickhauser's heads, smashing them flat, leaving their children, Vic and Mick, orphaned.

Mr. Stuffy said he was stifled without sunlight and he fled. Mrs. Stuffy became so distraught she ate her gingerbread house (with Mrs. Tubula's condolences and help), forcing her and her son to move into a tent made from throw rugs.

The mayor's office was overrun with cries for help. His advisors suggested he act quickly. After all, it was an election year.

Dot Dash telegraphed the message for another town hall meeting. The citizens of Yoosa, young and old, crowded onto wooden benches inside the hall. This time Yoosians didn't gab about their lives. All conversations were about the sun. Voices were strained. Tones were grumpy.

Percy and his family sat in the second row behind the imposing wall of Clumpies. Dilly perched at Percy's feet. Percy noticed Bard, the poetry farmer, standing in the shadows in a corner of the room. His shaggy hair flopped in his face as he scribbled on a piece of paper, erased what he wrote, scribbled some more, erased some more....

Mayor Oscar pounded on the podium with a new jumbo-size gavel Mr. Woodruff had carved for the occasion. "Attention, everyone! Quiet down! You all know why you're here, so I'll get right to the point since there's only one point on the agenda that I'd like to point out—"

"It's not polite to point," Mrs. Mortimer said.

"I hope his point isn't pointless," Needle-Nose Nelson said.

"Wake me up if he says anything important," Mr. Snozhead said.

"Anybody bring anything to eat?" Mrs. Tubula asked.

"QUIET!" The mayor smacked down the gavel. "Please, a little consideration! I know nerves are frayed and—"

"Frayed? I'm a big ball of nerves!"

"I'm a nervous wreck!"

"I've lost my nerve."

"Order in the hall!" THWACK! The gavel crashed again. The mayor's face steamed; his sausage nose boiled. The crowd hushed.

"First," Mayor Oscar said, "I have asked Yoosa's very own poetry farmer, Bard Leary, to read us one of his poems, to help us through this difficult time. Please lend him your ears. Bard?" The mayor motioned for him.

Bard shuffled to the podium, his head down. He looked as rumpled as the piece of paper he held. He cleared his throat, smoothed out the paper, and turned it right side up. He cleared his throat again.

"Ode on Summertime in Yoosa," Bard said. In a soft but clear voice, he recited:

> Shall I compare thee to a summer's day?
> I shant. I can't. Not enough sunlight today.
> So upon a daytime dreary
> While I pondered weak and weary
> All mimsy were the borogroves
> And not one of them was cheery.
> But O heart! Take heart!
> We can stop our hearts from breaking
> Between the dark and the daylight,
> And rage we must against the dying of light.
> Because even if your candle burns at both ends,
> It will not last the night.

Bard's voice grew louder. He straightened, looked into the crowd.

Yoosians, if we can keep our heads as the sun floats away,
Then that will make all the difference today!

Bard dropped his head.

Mrs. Veerance jumped up and clapped. "I loved it," she said to Mr. Veerance.

"Bravo, my fellow wordsmith!" Philious Mot said.

Bard scurried away from the podium.

A few people applauded, including Percy, Mrs. Mortimer, Turner Page, and, of course, Pat and Pat, whose favorite game was patty-cake. But most sat still.

"Sheesh, how does a poetry farmer make a living?" Rocky Cardia asked. "He's one *V* away from poverty."

"I wouldn't trade a box of matchsticks for that poem."

"Heck, I wouldn't trade two flies for it."

"I wouldn't trade one bobbypin."

"I wouldn't trade an inch of floss."

"Yoosa needs action, not words!"

Mayor Oscar returned to the podium. "I'm sure you'll all join me in thanking Bard for his inspirational poem; I truly hope he inspired you. Getting back to the compelling reason for this meeting, I'm looking for—"

Leaning forward, Percy stuck his head between two of the Clumpies. "May I interrupt, Mayor Oscar?"

"You already have."

"May I continue?

"You already are."

"Then, Your Honor..." Percy hesitated. The cowlick on his head flew up, then settled back down. He climbed through the Clumpies and

"Then, Your Honor..." Percy hesitated. The cowlick on his head flew up, then settled back down. He climbed through the Clumpies and faced the mayor. "I will go to the top of Amethyst Mountain," he said.

Mayor Oscar leaned over the podium and peered down his bulbous nose. "You'll do what?"

"I'm your volunteer."

Dilly clapped his paws together. Pat and Pat joined in. Some people gasped, others snickered.

"The poem wasn't *that* good," someone said.

The mayor looked puzzled. "You're volunteering to do what?"

"To secure the rope to the sun at the top of Amethyst Mountain," Percy said.

His parents froze like icicles. Peg cried. A hullabaloo broke out.

Mr. Clumpie guffawed. "But you're just a boy, and a runt of a one, I might add," he said. "A bad choice to go."

"And you're too quiet, sweetheart," Wanda Bovine said. "If you yelled for help, we couldn't hear you."

"You're too shy," Effie Ewing said.

"Too slow," Triple Jay said.

It seemed to Percy everyone had an opinion on the matter.

"You're not strong enough."

"Not aggressive enough."

"Not clever enough."

"You'll never succeed."

"You're too skinny."

"He is not," Midge Thinley said.

"You wear glasses."

Dilly growled. So did Cyril Klops.

Was it Percy's imagination, or was everyone extra mean tonight?

"It will take you days. You can't survive that long."

"The cloud spirit will guide him," Leo Hohokam said.

"Go play with your clay, Leo!"

"I thought no one was dumb enough, but I guess I was wrong!"

"You pick peas, for cryin' out loud!"

"Oh, for heaven's sake," Saffron Pepperaji said, "let him try."

"Why? He won't make it."

"Yes, I will," Percy said.

The hullabaloo was deafening.

"Hold it down!" shouted the mayor. "Now, Percy, I appreciate what you're trying to do, but what makes you think you can scale the mountain?"

Percy stood tall. "I can plod," he said.

Laughter filled the hall. Vance and Vera Veerance unthawed, turning to slush in their seats. Dilly wagged his ears. Percy smiled.

Eight

⊯►Percy Plods

TODAY WAS THE DAY! In semi-darkness, the Veerance family attempted to eat breakfast—barley cereal and yam jam on toasted lettuce leaves. Percy couldn't eat; he was too nervous. His parents weren't eating either. They stared at their plates. Mrs. Veerance folded and refolded her napkin. She wrinkled her eyebrows. Mr. Veerance scratched his head with a carrot stick. The only sound at the plank table was Peg, fussing. She clung to Percy's arm and refused to eat, even when Mrs. Veerance bribed her with pea pudding. Percy tried not to look at his family. A sudden feeling overwhelmed him: he would miss them. Good thing Dilly was coming along.

Percy read and reread the list of supplies for his trip. Don't forget anything! Except he didn't know for sure what he should take. Bring plenty of food, that much he knew. Hunger would make the trip harder.

In the pantry, he inventoried the shelves—not much good food to choose from. Into a knapsack he packed oat biscuits, a loaf of vegetable medley bread, candy-coated parsley, tomato cookies, dried egg-plant slices, baked carrot chips, chickpea fritters, squash pie, a jar of Yoosian spring water, and as a last resort, a handful of Brussels sprouts pops. It would be a bad day on the mountain if he and Dilly were forced to eat veggie pops. But better them than starvation. But surely that situation would never arise, would it?

He also included the plump frankfurter Mayor Oscar had brought by the previous evening. The mayor had wished Percy luck and thanked him for "giving me more time to figure out a real solution."

Percy did not pack the bag of crackers from Midge Thinley. They tasted like cardboard. She said they were indeed made from paper—so no calories! Peg would eat them.

Effie Ewing had brought Percy a wool sweater she had knitted herself. She looked sheepish as she apologized that the sweater wasn't finished. Her sheep weren't providing much fleece because of the lack of sunshine. Only the arms and collar sections were complete. Percy accepted it with thanks and packed it.

Vera Veerance had pulled Mrs. Ewing aside. "Does Percy going up the mountain seem like a good idea to you?" she asked, wrinkling her eyebrows.

"Sounds iffy," said Effie.

Percy packed the walking stick Udell Woodruff had made from a carved piece of oak. It had three hinges to make it fold in thirds. Percy didn't think he'd need it—he could plod fine all by himself—but he didn't want to hurt Mr. Woodruff's feelings by leaving it home. He also packed the enormous spool of dental floss dropped off by Buckminster Dent. "Don't lose your teeth, Perce. Wooden teeth don't work well at all, no matter how good Udell carves." Percy wasn't worried about his teeth, but the floss might come in handy.

He didn't pack the jar of pomade Mayor Oscar had given him to smooth down his cowlick. "Image is everything," the mayor had said. "You never know who you might meet on the mountain." Percy didn't care about an image. Neither did his cowlick.

"Here, Percy dear, take some of my fifteen-bean kabobs for your trip," Mrs. Veerance said. "I made them with navy beans, kidney beans, wax beans, pinto beans—"

"That's okay, Mom. My sack's getting full. Let Peg have them."

Peg lay on the floor, blubbering, kicking her chubby legs in the air. She threw a bottle of mushroom juice across the kitchen.

"Are you sure you have enough to eat?" asked Mrs. Veerance. "You're still a growing boy, aren't you? And if you do get hungry, you come straight home. I'll fix you a big plate of fried kale. Your favorite, isn't it?"

"No, Mom."

Mrs. Veerance's brow furrowed. "That's funny...your father loves it."

"You bet, Vera. How about frying up a batch for dinner tonight?"

Percy finished loading the backpack with a cup and two bowls, a wooden ball, a book, a bar of soap, a towel, salt and pepper shakers, bandages, two pairs of sunglasses, a rubber band, candles and matches, two blankets, and pencil and paper.

"What do you need sunglasses for?" asked Mr. Veerance. "There's barely a drop of sun in the sky."

"But there could be more. It could be really bright on top of the mountain."

Mr. Veerance rolled his eyes. "Egads, Percy, you sure about this? Nobody expects you, of all people, to go. Really, they don't."

"I'm sure I can plod."

"Even if you only make it partway and have to turn back, that's okay. The mayor will find someone else."

"Dad, I want to go. The sun's about gone."

"I don't think a ten-year-old boy should go," Mrs. Veerance said.

"I'm eleven, Mom."

"Really? My, how time flies." Her voice was shrill as she sang:

It's such a surprise to see how time flies.
In the wink of an eye, a month has gone bye-bye.
Before you know it, a year's passed again,
And the boy you thought was ten is really eleven!
She bop-a-loobba, ba ba bop-blooba...

"Beautiful, Vera," Mr. Veerance said. "I could listen to you sing all day."

Mrs. Veerance blushed.

"When did you say you are leaving?"

"Later today, Dad."

WHAAAA!" cried Peg. She crawled over to Percy and hung onto his leg.

"Oh, no, I can't go up the mountain now—I've got a Peg Leg!" Percy picked her up. "Don't worry, Peg. I'll be back in a few days. And I'll bring you a present. Something good to eat from Amethyst Mountain."

Peg gurgled. She slipped a slimy pea into Percy's hand, who slid it into his pants pocket.

"Don't forget to write thank-you notes for the gifts you received," Mrs. Veerance said.

"I won't. I brought pencil and paper."

"I have some advice for you, too," Mr. Veerance said.

"Yes, Dad?"

"Don't embarrass our family."

❊ ❊ ❊

On his way to Flora's farm, Percy stopped at Mona's stall. She looked droopier than usual. Percy gave her an oat biscuit. She gnashed it with her buck teeth. Percy combed her hair. "Auntie will be by to take care of you. I'll be back soon, old girl." Mona moaned.

❀ ❀ ❀

In Flora's buggy, Percy visited Yoosa farms one last time to help his aunt deliver flowers. Most of the farmers hadn't placed orders—with the sun almost gone, smelling roses was the last thing on their minds. But Flora brought bouquets by anyway. She wore her bonnet made of gladiolas—her "glad hat" as she called it, hoping to improve people's moods.

Percy said good-bye to Grandpap Gence. The crickets sang him a farewell song. He couldn't understand the cricket lyrics, but it sounded like a funeral hymn.

They stopped at Mr. Dent's farm so Dilly could say good-bye to Bruce, his moose friend.

"Hello, Miss Flora," Mr. Dent said. "I don't know which are more lovely—your bouquets or your teeth."

"Have a posy, Buckminster."

"When you return, Perce, I'll teach you about dental floss farming. You know, you don't have to be a vegetable farmer if you don't want to."

"I don't?"

"No, siree! I come from a long line of rack farmers—hats and coats. My ancestors made wall-mounted hat racks from elk and moose antlers. That's how I got Bruce. And when I contemplated what to do with his macrodontial condition, I conceived the bright idea about floss. And look where it got me! A huge improvement, personally and professionally speaking. How 'bout it, Perce. Want to learn the floss biz?"

Their final destination was Tom Fowler's farm. He'd ordered a fragrant bunch of carnations to put in the wild birds' cages (to entice them to lay more eggs). He traded the carnations for a basket of teriyaki vulture wings, two smoked turkey legs, an ostrich potpie, and a half dozen boiled pheasant eggs. Flora whispered to Percy, "You can take it all on your trip." Percy drooled like his little sister in front of a bowl of peas.

"Flora, I have another order," Tom Fowler said. "A bunch of forget-me-nots, if you please. And Percy, I think you're making a big mistake."

That made it almost unanimous. Except for Grandpap, everyone they'd seen that day told Percy he would not succeed. Chester Hardwicke said he'd more likely lasso a lightning bolt than rope in the sun. Vic Brickhauser said Percy had a bigger blockhead than he did. Rocky Cardia said a donkey had more brains. Bronco Snozhead said Percy took after his father. (Dilly had growled at them all.)

Percy rubbed his forehead. Was he being stupid? He sat silently on the buggyride back to Flora's cottage.

"Don't listen to Tom Fowler," she said, "or any of the others. They don't know you like I do, and I know you'll make it. All set to go?"

"Ready as I'll ever be."

Flora gave Dilly a package of cow bones for their trip. His ears wagged from side to side. Then she gave Percy the biggest hug ever.

Percy felt a pang. No time for doubt now. He shuffled his feet. "There's a fresh batch of bean kabobs at my house, Auntie. Better hurry over and get some."

Flora laughed. "I see Vera Veerance, V.C.S. is at it again."

Percy sighed.

"Want me to walk with you partway?" asked Flora.

Percy stalled before replying, "No, I'm fine."

"Ruff!"

"One last thing, Percy. There's a wise woman who lives next to Zeal Crater, halfway up the mountain. Her name is Ima. She's an old friend. If you need help, find her. You can't miss the crater. It's a big hole in the ground. And remember what I told you...."

❋ ❋ ❋

With the last flecks of daylight lighting the way, Percy and Dilly hiked through the backwoods of Yoosa, around Lake Cheery, and then plodded up the brownish-green foothills. At the base of Amethyst Mountain, they stopped before a narrow vertical path. There they set up camp for the night. They ate a candlelight dinner of vulture, eggplant, and spring water. "So far, so good, Dilly," Percy said, munching on a roasted wing the size of his forearm. "More vulture?"

"Ruff!"

"After dinner I'll read you a chapter from my book. It's about—" Percy heard a flapping sound. Louder and louder it became, sounding like a bundle of umbrellas opening and closing quickly. It grew louder still, until it sounded like an army of flying elephants. Percy's cowlick jumped up. A torrent of wind knocked his glasses off. Dilly ducked under a blanket. Something mammoth swooped down from the sky. A spear whizzed by Percy's head. Through the flapping sound, Percy heard a barbaric yawp. It sounded like *"Groistayoba!"* He crawled over to the lump in the blanket and crouched over Dilly. He covered his head with his arms. At last the sound faded.

"Whew, what the heck was that?!" Percy retrieved his glasses. Dilly stuck his head out from the blanket. "Did you see it, Dilly? It was enormous!"

Was that Grizzman? Grizzman couldn't fly, could he? Whoever it was better be gone for good. Percy didn't discuss Grizzman thoughts with Dilly—didn't want to scare him. Percy tried to shake off his fear. "How 'bout if I read to you, Dilly? It's a really good story, about a flamingo named Nish who gets blown by a hurricane to this place called Walden Pond where there are greedy ducks and—"

Snort! "Zzzzzz...."

The next morning, day number one on Amethyst Mountain, Percy was ready for action. "Let the adventure begin!"

"Ruff!"

Before them a broken sign stuck in the ground. Percy read aloud because Dilly couldn't read. "'Walk of Miser.' Hmmm, I wonder who the miser is? Maybe he knows a shortcut to the mountain peak."

Dilly pawed Percy's foot. Percy looked down and picked up a broken piece of the sign—the letter Y. Attaching the piece to the sign, he read aloud again, "Walk of Misery." He gulped.

All day they plodded uphill. The path cut through trenches and troughs, wandered into gullies, gulches, and gutters, and dipped into culverts and pits. Whoever had designed the path must have had a shabby streak as wide as these ditches. It was designed for misery all right! The backpack weighed heavily on Percy's back. The supply sack dug into his shoulder. His legs ached. Soon his pace slowed. As the sun faded altogether, Percy's body felt as if he'd been run over by his dad's vegetable cart.

"Are you as dog-tired as me?" he said to Dilly.

Dilly panted; his tongue scraped the ground.

"I never knew misery could be so miserable. Plodding is not as easy as it sounds, but at least we've made progress. A little farther, then we'll camp."

Blackness fell around them, hampering their sight. They stumbled into boulders and tripped over rocks. The only thing Percy could think to do was keep plodding, keep plodding. They followed the path around a bend, which abruptly ended on a slippery slope. Percy lost his balance, fell on his butt, and began sliding downward. Dilly skidded on his backside next to him.

The slope narrowed into a chute. They twisted around curves, picking up speed. Zooming ahead, all Percy could see was a dark blur. In an instant, they flew off the end of the chute and catapulted through the air. KERPLUNK! They landed in a pool of gooey brown stuff.

"P.U.! Where are we? A Poo Pool? This place smells worse than the compost heap!"

Dilly grunted.

Percy held the backpack and knapsack above his head as they slowly sank in the quagmire. It was too dark to see the edge of the pool. "Dog-paddle, Dilly. I can't tell which way to swim. We'll have to wait until morning to see which way we can get out. Keep your paws moving."

Percy sank to his waist. He struggled to take the walking stick from his backpack. He held it out for Dilly, who wrapped his paws around one end. Percy saw the exhaustion in Dilly's eyes as the dog rested its head on the walking stick. Soon Dilly's eyes shut and Percy heard the familiar "Zzzzz...."

Percy sank to his shoulders. He kicked his legs to stay afloat. He yawned, watched Dilly sleep. He was not about to let anything happen to his dog, especially since it was the first day of their trip!

As the night wore on, Percy held onto the stick and packs. He tried to think of fun things instead of worrying about the stinky mess he had gotten them into. In the distance, he heard the same flapping sound as the previous night. Was that *"Groistayoba!"* again? Almost completely submerged, Percy wiggled back and forth. How can you plod when you can barely move?

He yawned. Stay awake... don't drown... stay awake... don't drown....

Nine

◄— Valter Vulture

PERCY NODDED OFF AND DREAMT he was standing on the mountaintop next to a sleeping bear. Was it friendly? The bear woke up and growled, its sharp teeth glistening like a saw blade—a glistening spark of sunlight awakened Percy. He looked around and groaned. Day two on the mountain—and stuck in the middle of a putrid pool, far from the edge. One good thing, at least no bears could get him.

Dilly snoozed with his head resting on the walking stick. Percy could barely move his legs. His arm was frozen in place from holding the walking stick all night. He needed to figure a way out fast. "P.U.!" he yelled in frustration.

Dilly mumbled a ruff.

"Hey, Dilly. Sorry to wake you up. In case you're wondering, we're still stuck."

A warm gust of wind blew them closer to the pool's edge. Then another burst of wind. And another. If the wind kept blowing, it could blow them all the way to the shore, and they could get out.

But the wind stopped as a dark cloud passed overhead. Percy heard a loud flapping sound. Oh, no, the flying elephants were coming! His cowlick shot straight up. Instead of elephants in the sky, he saw an elephantine beak. The beak belonged to a vulture as big as a Clumpie Brother, but dressed much better. It sported a top hat, bow tie, and a velvet vest with gold buttons. The vulture hovered over them, opened its hooked beak, and spit out a bundle of spears. One nicked Dilly's ear. He yelped.

"Stop it!" Percy tried to wave the vulture away.

"No boy shall tell me what to do," it said. Another spear zinged from its beak, whizzing between Percy and Dilly.

"Hold it," Percy said. "What did the porcupine say to the turtle?"

"I, Valter Vulture, do not care." He touched down on the shore. "Vacky humans. *Groistayoba!*"

Percy observed Valter Vulture with curiosity: his featherless head, neck, and legs, and the large hole in its beak. No vultures lived in Yoosa. Only Mr. Fowler captured them.

"No time for joking when you've been swamped in Stinko Swamp," Valter said.

"Could you please help us?"

"Vhy should I?"

"Because we need it."

"Vhat your name? Vhere you from?"

"I'm Percy Veerance, from Yoosa."

"I know Yoosa. A vacky bird hunter there, no haberdashery. I stay avay. Vhat you doing here?"

"We're climbing to the mountaintop."

"You're in middle of swamp, can't move, but you think you can climb up the mountain? Yoosians are crazy creatures."

"I didn't mean to end up in the swamp. I was following a walk and—"

"Not the Valk of Misery? *Groistayoba!* You are crazy!"

"No, I'm not crazy. Why are you spitting spears at us? That's not exactly normal."

"Those aren't spears, they are poles. I come from the Land of Poles. That's vhat ve do vhen ve don't like something. Throw poles. Vorks better than throwing tantrums."

"What don't you like about me?

"You vrankle me."

"Vhat do you mean? I mean, what do you mean?"

"Vhat you think? I don't like to see you eating the wings of my vulture relatives. Very vrude."

"Ohhh...." Percy sank lower into the swamp. "I hadn't thought about it."

"You not think? Vhat is vrong with you? You cannot go through life not thinking!"

"You're right, Mr. Vulture. But could you please not spit poles at us?"

"Ruffff!"

"Ah, the brown fuzzy pickle talks?" Valter said.

"It's not a pickle. He's my dog, Dilly."

"A dog vit glasses? Dogs don't vear glasses."

"Mine does."

"Funny-looking dog you have, Mr. Percy. In Land of Poles, we haf sausage look more like dog than him!"

Dilly growled.

"Hush, you vruff-vruff," Valter said. "Don't be a buttinski."

"What's a buttinski?" Percy asked.

"Annoying creatures, like my in-laws."

"Can you help us, give us a lift out of here?"

"I should like to inform you that life is full of stinky swamps. Von must learn to get out of them by vonself."

"Well, sometimes one needs help," Percy said. "It's okay to ask for help."

"True," Valter said.

"Does that mean you'll help us?"

"Perhaps. If you eat relatives of something else, like geese. Make horrible sound. Honk honk honk! *Groistayoba!* Festers my feathers! Geese vorth getting vrid of."

"How about turkey? We could eat them."

"Ah, that make me vrapturous vraptor! Valter not care about gobblers. No vrelation to me. Although my in-laws do gobble a lot."

"Mr. Vulture, we promise never to eat vulture again. And I mean *never,* if you help us out."

"A good thing for you I have vonderful vay about me. Or you two be stinky drowned creatures soon." Valter removed his top hat and set it down. He swooped over Dilly, clamped onto Dilly's ear with his beak, and dragged him out of the swamp. He flung Dilly onto the shore. Covered in gunk, Dilly tried to scrape it off with his paws.

Then Valter gripped onto Percy's neck with his talons.

"Oww!"

Valter tugged harder, pumped his broad wings. He pulled Percy above the surface and dropped him swampside.

"Oww!" Percy said, landing on his rear. He tried to wipe the crud off his clothes. "Thank you, Mr. Vulture. I'm thankful for your help."

"And I am glad you have manners. They must have spread to other parts. They originated in the Land of Poles, like the vriting of thank-you letters. Ve call it being Pole-ite. Never underestimate the power of Pole-iteness. In Land of Poles, ve have saying, 'Vrudeness get you in deep doo-doo. Pole-iteness get you out.'"

"My Auntie Flora would like that saying. She has one that says, 'A kind word turns away wrath.'"

"Your aunt sounds pole-ite."

"May I please ask one more favor, Mr. Vulture?"

"Yes, since you askcd so pole-itely."

"Can you tell us the easiest way to get to the mountaintop?"

"Vhy you vant to go there?"

"To rope the sun back in."

"Ah, a grand purpose. How commendable." Valter pointed his wing to a forest in the distance. "For the best way, follow the Trail of Trees."

"IIow will I know which way to go?"

"My friends in the Song Brigade will guide you."

"Who are they?"

"Birds who sing."

"How will I find them?"

"Listen for their tune."

"One more thing I'm curious about," Percy said. "Why does Stinko Swamp smell so bad?"

"You've never heard of Bo Corpus?"

"No, what is it?"

"It's a he. He possessed very bad body odor, vorst in the vorld. If you got too close, his stench could melt your skin."

"How did he get to smell so bad?"

"Partly from the fact that he wouldn't bathe, vhich, by the vay, is very bad manners. But mostly it was from Bo's stinky personality. The combination was badly offensive. He was called 'B.O. Bo.' One day while fishing in Clear Lake, B.O. Bo's stink drove the fish wild. They jumped up and down in the vater and the vaves capsized his boat. He drowned and his decaying body polluted the lake. No more fish. It's been called Stinko Swamp ever since. Proving once more that bad manners will get you in deep doo-doo."

Great story, Percy thought.

Valter tipped his hat. "Delightful meeting you, Percy. I apologize for nicking your dog's ear, but I vas only trying to scare you. I would never poke you with a sharp object. That's not pole-ite. And now, I am off. Shall we meet again, call me Valter. And be careful on your travels. A monster lives near the mountaintop. A very bad-mannered monster." With a whoosh of his powerful wings, Valter disappeared into the gray sky.

Percy watched him fly out of sight. "Let's find the Song Brigade, Dilly, but first, a stream. We need to bathe. Don't want to end up like B.O. Bo."

Ten

Blue J. Magpie and Pinkolo DeLark

CLEAN AND REFRESHED, Percy and Dilly rested by a bubbly-bath brook. In the shade of willow trees, they munched on vegetable medley bread and Mayor Oscar's sausage. Percy took inventory of their food and was relieved it hadn't been contaminated by Stinko Swamp. He calculated they had enough for four more days—plenty to last the trip.

Percy heard a grating sound, like a wagon scraping across gravel. He found the source of the noise: a dark blue bird perched above them. It cawed and hawed as it sang:

> Poor poor pitiful me,
> Everything sad happens to me.
> Life is depressing as can be.
> What am I to do? Boo hoo hoo.
>
> c

The willow trees wept. The sound pricked Percy's skin. "Excuse me, Mr. Blue Crow—"

"The name's Blue J. Magpie, if it's any concern of yours, Mack," answered the bird in a gravelly voice. A black beret was cocked on the side of its head.

"Are you part of the Song Brigade?"

"What's it to ya, pal?"

"Can you lead us through the Trail of Trees?"

"You sure you want to follow me? I'm in the middle of a bummed-out ballad, Bub."

"That's okay. You sing. We'll follow."

"Suit yourself, Junior. And what's with the fuzzy brown caterpillar?" Dilly growled.

"It's not a caterpillar. He's a dog."

"A dog without a tail. That guy oughta be singin' the blues like me!"

Warbling a melancholy tune, the magpie flew from tree to tree. Percy and Dilly plodded behind. The low-lying branches blocked the sunlight and swatted them as they passed.

As the Trail of Trees became denser and darker, Blue J. Magpie's song became grimmer. Percy and Dilly covered their ears. The singing jangled their nerves.

They entered an orchard of brambly trees. Spiny leaves jabbed at them. The air was stifling, making it difficult to breathe.

"Mr. Magpie, please wait up," Percy said. "This is a terrible path."

"Well, boo hoo to you, Mr. Glum Chum. I'm singing the blues, Bud. Whaddja expect, the sunny side of the street? You're following the road of gloom and doom."

"Are you always so gloomy?"

"Family business—pessimism."

Even vegetablism was better than that. "Any chance you can lead us on a more pleasant path?"

"Crazy, man. You've picked the wrong bunch of feathers. You need pink birds for that. They're involved in a whole different line of work: accentuating the positive, sprinkling joy around, that kind of guano. Revolting! Personally, I can't abide cheeriness. Sticks in my craw."

"Where can we find a pink bird?"

"One will be by soon. You wait long enough, things get better. Too bad for me. Ta ta, time for me to hit the road, Jack. Don't let the merriment get you, and man, oh, man, beware of Grizzman!" Blue J. hopped away muttering, "Woe is I, too depressed to fly."

At least the magpie had good grammar. Its singing reminded Percy of his mom. He felt a pinch of sadness. Blue J.'s mood was infectious. *Poor, poor Percy, so forlorn am I....*

Percy and Dilly continued by themselves through the jabbing trees, not knowing where they were going. Just when Percy thought the gloom would never end, a sweet tune filled the air. "Listen!" he said. The melody sounded like, *How Much is that Doggie in the Window?* one of Percy's favorite songs. A good sign. Percy's mood lightened. Then a pink bird with a yellow derby flitted by.

"Excuse me, Mr. Pink Bird. Are you part of the Song Brigade?"

"Affirmative, young fellow. I'm Pinkolo DeLark, an official Cheery Chirper. "

"I'm Percy from Yoosa, and this is my dog, Dilly."

"Cute doggie."

"Thanks. Can we follow you out of the forest?"

"Positively."

"Bobbydazzler!"

"You need a spry step and a sunny disposition. Strut on, chaps!" He sang in a larky fashion:

O rhapsodic day, think pink and say,
Life is like a cherry bowl, deep and sweet,
Move your feet, let the good times roll....

"Follow that song, Dilly!"

Time flew by as Pinkolo lead them on a happier route. His chippy chirping motivated Percy. Plodding seemed effortless. Percy and Dilly enjoyed watching Pinkolo toss his derby in the air and then catch it back on his head.

Later in the day they came upon a lively orchard. The trees swayed in time to Pinkolo's song. Percy clapped along with the trees. Dilly's ears swung to the beat. Fresh air swept through the orchard. Percy felt invigorated. He was glad he'd come to Amethyst Mountain!

Next they proceeded through a Bird of Paradise grove. A chorus of pink birds joined in song, providing an exhilarating accompaniment to their plodding. Percy and Dilly bopped along.

The grove ended near a canyon. "Oh, rhapsodic day! We're here, merry men," Pinkolo said, pointing to a sign: "Honey Tears Gulch." "This is as far as I go. Hike down the canyon, then follow the path on the other side."

"Thanks for leading us, Mr. DeLark. That was fun!"

"Positively."

"By the way," Percy said, "do you know why Stinko Swamp smells so bad?"

"Legend says that's where a faction of the Song Brigade, called the Mournful Minstrels, deposited their rotten eggs for many generations. The Minstrels grieved themselves to death, but their legacy reeks on. And on that note, have a pleasant journey. And remember, think pink!"

Beats *"Groistayoba!"* Percy thought.

They plodded into Honey Tears Gulch. Percy hoped it would be more honey than tears, but it wasn't. Along the way, the ground changed from dirt to cobblestone, to pumice, then granite. The gulch eroded Percy's good mood. His feet hurt as if he'd been walking barefoot on a pile of Vic Brickhauser's crushed bricks. He wished he had a pair of Scoot Boots, but this was not the time for wishful thinking. He had to think pink, concentrate on plodding. Percy looked behind the rocks for honey—a nice treat to have with their biscuits. But he couldn't find any. The sky darkened; they trudged on.

In pitch-black darkness, parched and exhausted, Percy and Dilly reached the other side of the canyon. Percy said they would look for the new path in the morning. He pulled off his shoes and socks, winced at his blistered feet. "Now I know why the path was named for tears."

Dilly howled.

"Your pups hurt, too?" Percy bandaged the cuts on Dilly's paws. "You'll be fine tomorrow, Dill," he said in a think-pink voice.

How much farther to the top? Percy felt beat. The effort of the last two days weighed on him. Everything hurt, even his hair. Maybe he shouldn't have volunteered. Maybe it was a dumb idea.

Silently, they ate ostrich potpie. On the hard ground, Dilly fell asleep gnawing on a cow bone. Percy fell asleep thinking about turning back and going home. He dreamed that he plodded to the front door of his house. Dilly was gone, he didn't know where. With dread in his stomach, he opened the door, his cowlick hanging in his face. His parents stood like tin soldiers glaring at him. Peg crawled to him, pounded on his foot, and crawled away.

"You're a failure," Mr. Veerance said.

"Why did you even bother?" Mrs. Veerance said.

"We knew you couldn't do it."

"You've embarrassed yourself."

"Egads! You've embarrassed all of us."

Eleven

Droll Troll

P ERCY WOKE UP STARTLED. He squirmed, tried to fall back to sleep, but couldn't. He sat up, spread his blanket over Dilly, and watched him sleep. He rubbed his arms to stay warm and waited for a speck of sunlight to announce another morning—day three of their journey.

❋ ❋ ❋

Back in Yoosa, people talked nonstop about Percy and his high-falutin' attempt to climb the mountain. It gave them a new topic to discuss other than the faltering sunlight and their faltering Mayor. Yoosians laughed at the idea of Percy's thinking he could fix the sun problem.

The Pettifog Fogies, senior citizens who sat on a park bench classifying the color of the sky, invented a new game: the Percy Odds. They posted their data on the bulletin board in the town rhomboid.

The odds of Percy making it back down the mountain
in any condition: 100 to 1.
The odds of Percy fixing the sun: 1,000 to 1.
The odds of Dilly leaving Percy behind and
returning alone: 100,000 to 1.
The odds of Mr. Veerance going after his son
and bringing him home: 1,000,000 to 1.

Mr. and Mrs. Veerance avoided going to town.

Percy spied a smidgen of sunlight. *Time to rise—and shine?* He moved like a tinman with rusted joints. He hobbled around investigating where they were. He found another sign: "Stroll of Droll." It was a narrow path cutting through bristly vegetation. Lined with weeds, it looked flat and smooth.

Percy petted Dilly until he woke up. Dilly yawned, muffled a "Ruff."

"Here's our plan today," Percy said. "Imagine we're walking through a field of soft clover and the cool grass soothes our feet. Doesn't that sound good?"

Dilly managed a more enthusiastic ruff.

They plodded along the Stroll past patches of milkweed, duckweed, and ragweed. The weeds gave off a funky odor, like fermenting grains in Uncle Linus's silo. Percy sneezed over and over. Too bad he didn't have one of Uncle Linus's hankies.

In the afternoon, the air turned crisp and smelled of sage.

Tumbleweeds cropped up forcing Percy and Dilly to bend around them. As they continued along, the path became even more narrow as the tumbleweeds became bigger. The path finally ended in a blockade of tumbleweeds ten feet high and ten feet wide. "We can't get through this," Percy said. "What we need is a big gust of wind to blow them—"

As if he had issued a command, a burst of warm wind blew through the middle of the blockade, leaving a hole large enough to crawl through. Percy and Dilly wasted no time.

On the other side was an embankment. Below it an aquamarine river rushed by, making a hissing sound. A ramp led to an enormous iron bridge stretching over the river. Percy marveled at the bridge's lattice structure, delicate as lace. It looked like a spiderweb floating in the sky. An ornamental gate blocked the entrance to the bridge. Percy jiggled it, but the handle was locked.

"How can we get across this bridge, Dilly? It's too high to climb up."

Dilly blew hard.

"I don't think the wind can blow open this gate. We need the key. I wonder where it is."

From under the bridge, a corpulent creature—bigger than the Clumpie Brothers—with buggy lime green eyes, stubby teeth, and a chin to match, scaled the embankment lickety-split. Percy jumped back. His cowlick jumped, too. Dilly growled.

The creature galumphed toward Percy. "Hullo! Hullo!" it yelled.

Percy and Dilly scrambled down the embankment and hid in a ravine.

"Hullo, lads! Where'd you run off to?"

Lying on his belly, Percy cautiously lifted his head for a peek. The right side of the creature's face and body were covered in bristly weeds. The left side was smooth. On top of his head, a mop of thistles twisted like a pretzel. He was covered in a layer of dried mud.

"Come back, won't you? Care to play?"

Play? The creature seemed less frightening.

"The name's Mr. Droll Troll. Be pleased to make your acquaintance. Hullo, there, can you hear me?"

Percy stood and said, "Hi." Dilly popped out of the ravine. Both gawked at the creature.

"Whimsey woo, a human!" The creature smiled like a gargoyle.

Percy's eyes darted back and forth from Droll's bristly right side to his smooth left side.

Droll blushed (on the left side). "I see you've noticed my bristles. Sorry for the unsightly sight, but when you live on the ground, you get plant-bound. I've become a host for unruly vegetation and as a result, can't bathe often. Don't want to water the plants."

Percy thought Valter would not approve.

"You get used to it," Droll Troll said, "long as you have sharp shears. I was right in the middle of landscaping myself when I heard clatter out here. I was so excited to have company to frolic with that I ran out to see who was calling and didn't have time to finish trimming."

A blaring sound rumbled from beneath the bridge. *"DDRRROLLL!!"*

The bridge shook. Percy's and Dilly's glasses rattled.

"Och! Whimsey poo!"

Percy looked around nervously. "What was that?"

"My wife, Tootsie. Just act like you don't hear her."

How can you ignore that voice?

"'Tis hard for a lad to have a little fun around here, Mister —?"

"Percy Veerance. From Yoosa."

"And a whimsey welcome to you, Mister Veerance! May I call you Percy? Excellent, a new friend."

Tootsie bellowed again. The ground quaked.

"Disregard her," Droll said. "And what's that?" He pointed at Dilly. "Looks like a sawed-off log."

Dilly growled.

"Didn't know a log could growl."

"It's not a log. He's my dog."

"I know," Droll said. "I was spoofing, trying to have a little fun. But he does have tree stump legs. And you're probably thinking that I look like a weed patch. So I know how he feels. What's his name?" Droll patted Dilly on the head. Dilly turned rigid. "A grand pooch. Could I trade you something for him?"

"No, thanks."

"Need any iron implements? A dagger, a saber, a claw?"

"No." Percy guessed not many Yoosa farmers would trade with him, except the hatchet farmer, Mr. Borden.

"Och! I need a playmate. Help me out, mate. Aren't we friends?"

"It takes longer than ten minutes to make a friend."

"'Tis lonely here, not a soul to play with. All I have is the missus. Not much fun. I built the bridge so I could escape, but Tootsie keeps dragging me back."

At that moment Tootsie screamed, "DROLL, GET BACK HERE OR I'LL BITE YOUR NOSE OFF!"

Percy froze. Dilly was still rigid.

"She's done that before. Talk about a troll. Took months to grow back. Can I please have your dog?"

"No! I'd never give Dilly away."

"Pretty please? Prettiest please in the world?!"

"NO!"

"Double poo!"

"Droll, we can't stay and play. We have to cross your bridge, then climb to the mountaintop."

Droll whooped with laughter. Chunks of mud fell off his body. "The top of the mountain? Och! You're good as dead, laddie."

"Why?"

"Haven't you heard of Grizzman?"

"Yes, but I'm trusting he won't bother us because we won't bother him. Have you encountered him?"

"No, but Tootsie has. Says he's a ghastly beast who could tear you to shreds in one swipe. She's deathly afraid of him. Sometimes I threaten her that I'll get Grizzman to play with me, and she shrivels in the sludge and leaves me alone. 'Tis dangerous what you're trying to do. You'll never make it."

Percy automatically said, "I can plod."

"Whimsey woo, that's funny. Listen, I have a great idea. Why don't you go by yourself and leave Dilly with me? You wouldn't put him in harm's way, would you?"

"We're inseparable. And we both have to cross your bridge."

"No one crosses my bridge."

"Why not?"

"Not until you play with me."

"Why?"

"So I can have fun," Droll said. "It's my bridge. I get to make the rules."

"Okay," Percy said cautiously. "If that's the only way. What shall we play?"

"A guessing game. If you answer my question correctly, you can cross."

"What happens if I answer wrong?"

"I keep Dilly and you depart."

"That's not a good deal."

"It's better than if I gave you to Tootsie. Accept my offer, or go back where you came from."

"Is your question a fill-in-the-blank, multiple choice, or true-false?"

"It's either-or."

"How many guesses do I get?"

Droll roared. "That's funny. Do I look like a dumb creature to you? Okay, so I have thistles growing out of my head. But they're not a dunce cap! This is a challenge. You're nothing unless you face challenges. Do you agree to my terms?"

Percy looked to Dilly for advice. Dilly wagged his ears. Percy hesitated, then said, "What's your question, Droll?"

"In one hand, I hold the key to unlock the gate. Which one is it?" Droll held out a coarse, bristly hand. "Is it this one?" Then he held out the left hand, which had been trimmed. "Or this one?"

Percy walked around Droll, examined his hands from every angle, and tried to determine if one hand bulged more than the other. Dilly pawed at his foot. "I can't hurry, Dill. If I guess incorrectly, I'll lose you." Percy studied both hands. Smooth or bristly? Hmmm...The bristly right hand appeared to bulge. Maybe that was because it had a key in it? Or maybe that was a trick and the bulging hand did NOT have the key?

"Och! Whimsey poo! I can't stand here all day," Droll said. "What's your answer?"

"Can I feel each hand?"

"No! Just guess!"

"I p-p-pick—"

Before Percy could answer, Tootsie crawled out from under the bridge and snuck up behind Droll, who couldn't see her. Neither could Percy, since Droll blocked Percy's view.

But Dilly saw her—hideous face and all. He howled like he'd never howled before. "RRRUUFFF!"

Droll grinned at Dilly—from bristly right ear to smooth left ear. "You're right, log dog! The key's in my rough hand." He uncurled his knobby fingers; a cast-iron key lay in his palm.

Percy picked up Dilly. "Dill, you're a champ! What a great dog!" Dilly continued to bark like crazy at Tootsie, who continued to stealthily sneak up on Droll.

With her gnarly hands, Tootsie yanked the thistles on Droll's head. He let out a thunderous cry. His neck snapped back. His eyes bulged out even more, looking like spinning marbles. Then he staggered backward, finally revealing Tootsie to Percy.

Percy came face to face with the reason Dilly was still barking like crazy. He gasped at the sight of her. Huge porcine body, legs like wooly ham hocks, piggish face with a nose like a boar, and spiky chin whiskers. Hedges grew from her head like tangled green tentacles. A real hedgehog!

So strong was Tootsie that she pulled Droll off his feet and began dragging him away. "Och poooooo...."

"What about the key?" Percy yelled. "Droll, the key, please!"

"Hope we're still friends!" Droll flung the key in the air. Dilly leapt and caught it in his mouth.

CRASH! Droll and his Tootsie disappeared under the bridge.

Twelve

Natsy Gnat

AFTER CROSSING DROLL'S BRIDGE, Percy and Dilly found another path with another sign: "Harsh Marsh." Percy got his wish—a soft surface. Plodding became sloshing in the mushy soil. They slogged uphill as fast as they could, to get as far away from Tootsie as possible.

As the sun faded, the air turned frigid. Weary, they stopped for the night in a bog. Percy lit candles and counted out their meal: one chickpea fritter, three carrot chips, a piece of dried eggplant, and two tomato cookies each. Dinner was consumed in minutes. Dilly looked just as hungry as before. Percy gave him a cow bone.

Together they snuggled in a bed of damp sedge. Percy laid his head on a clump of soggy ferns. He listened to Dilly snort, then snore. The candles flickered...

❀ ❀ ❀

Percy felt even more wetness as something splashed on his nose. Was it morning already, day number four? More sleep, please. Something dribbled down his cheek. Did he have to get up now? Did something lick his face? Who could sleep under these conditions? He opened his eyes, peered straight into the beady yellow orbs of—what was that!? Tootsie? Percy jumped up.

It wasn't Tootsie, but another creature staring at him. This one had dark circles around sunken eyes, a long tapered snout, a furry face, and a snarky smile with fang-like teeth. Its elfish body was dressed in a puffy shirt and baggy trousers. It wore a cone-shaped hat, like a court jester from stories of olden days. It was the size of a small boy, but it wasn't completely human. Percy had no idea what it was. He rubbed his eyes. Maybe he was dreaming.

"Heehaaw, youse alive," said *the thing,* slurping a wad of spit, which had trickled from its mouth. "I thought youse wuz dead, cuz you shure sleeped like youse wuz dead."

"I was tired." Percy watched the thing drool, in dire need of one of Uncle Linus's handkerchiefs.

"Whadder youse doin' on my property?" it said in a slushy voice.

"Sleeping," Percy said. "You own the marsh?"

"I own the eating rights. Whose you be?"

"I'm Percy from Yoosa. Who are you?"

"Natsy Gnat."

"Are you related to a gnat?"

"Heehaaw!" Natsy held onto his knees, laughing. "Everybody asks me that." Spit dripped from his mouth and puddled on the ground. "Not a gnat biologically," he said, "but psychologically. Annoying as one, youse might say."

"Like a buttinski?"

Natsy slurped. "No, an elfoon. We's a cross between elf and raccoon, a gluttonous breed related to the buffoon family, only trickier."

"I see the raccoon resemblance around the eyes," Percy said.

"All elfoon families originate from one of two lineages—either the
tatty or the natty."

"And you're from—"

"The natty side, of course." A string of saliva hung inches past
Natsy's chin. It swayed back and forth. Natsy removed his hat and
took out a fork and knife stored in the brim. "Never go anywhere without utensils. For us elfoons, it's always supper time—morning, noon,
night, and in-between!" He heehaaaawed, swallowed a mouthful of
spit. "We eat just about anything—and lots of it." Natsy poked a
sleeping Dilly with a fork. "What's that? A loaf of pumpernickel
bread?"

Dilly jumped up, growled at Natsy.

"It's not a loaf of bread. He's my dog."

"Harrumph! Bet I could make canine croutons out of him." Slurp.

Percy stuffed the blankets in his backpack and slung it over his
shoulder. He scooped up the knapsack and Dilly at the same time.
"Nice to meet you, Natsy, but we have to be going."

"Won't you stay for a meal?"

"Not today," Percy said. He was hungry, but dining with Natsy
could not be a pleasant experience. "Do you know a path to the top of
the mountain?"

"Why soitainly. You've come to the right elfoon. See that Duper
Tree way over there? Stand on the right side, then take one super-
duper step forward."

"Then which way?" Percy asked.

"Straight down. Uhh, I mean straight ahead."

Percy plodded off, looked back, saw Natsy rubbing his tiny paws together, saliva dripping from his chin. Percy plodded faster to the tree and positioned himself on the right side. He stretched out one leg and stepped forward into a pile of leaves. The leaves collapsed and he fell into a deep pit, landing with a thud on his butt. Dilly bounced out of his arms and smacked into the wall. The sandy walls crumbled in Percy's hands when he tried to crawl up them. Dilly tried crawling out, too, but slid back down.

"Help!" Percy said. "Natsy, can you hear me? We're stuck!"

Natsy scampered to the booby-trap pit and looked in. "That's the point."

"You tricked us?"

Slurp! "That's my job."

"Terrible job you have, Natsy, fooling people for a living," Percy said.

"It works for me. As I said, elfoons eat anything. And I'm starving." Natsy smirked. "Peoples and pooches is better 'n nuthin'. Boy oh boy, boy-doggie stew!"

Percy crouched in a corner. He held Dilly tightly in his arms and pressed him against his chest to stop his heart from beating so fast. *Think! How can we get out of here?*

Percy had an idea. From his backpack, he took out the enormous spool of dental floss and the wooden ball. He wrapped the floss tightly around the ball and as hard as he could, heaved it out of the pit. The floss made a whirring sound as it unraveled. An escape route! Using the floss like a piece of rope, Percy began climbing up the wall. He had made it halfway when he heard a loud "Harrumph!" The dental floss spool flew over Percy's head, and he fell backward onto the pit floor.

"Don't try to trick a trickster!"

Plan A had failed. What was Plan B? Percy listened to Natsy scurrying around the pit. He heard water pouring into a container (which he found out later was a vat the size of a bathtub). Percy called out, "Did you know I'm called a bean pole, and bean pole boys don't taste very good?"

"I eat trash," Natsy said. "How much worse can youse be? I even ate the old shoes from the last guy who came by. Saved a piece of the heel, makes a tangy spice."

"Natsy, what did the alligator say to the crocodile?"

"I'm not hungry for jokes."

"If you're so hungry, why don't you eat the eggs in Stinko Swamp?"

"They's no eggs in Stinko Swamp!"

"Yes, there are."

"You can't trick a trickster. They's only quadragasserts."

"Quadra*desserts?*" Percy asked.

"Not quadraDESSERTS. QuadraGASserts. Youse can't eat 'em, or youse'd be blowed up! They's worser than dried plums. Nobody eats quadragasserts, not even elfoons!"

"What are they?"

"Everyone knows that. Are you being tricky?"

"No, I'm being curious.

Natsy stacked wood around the vat. "They're tiny aquatic animals, from the nincompoop family, only with gills. They feed on scum at the bottom of the swamp. In the aft position, they have four holes for protection from predators."

"How do they protect themselves?"

"Can't you guess?

"I don't like guessing games."

"When they're scared, they blast scum gas out their aft holes! Heehaaw, heehaaaw! Pewie! Knocks you out! That's what makes the swamp smell so wretched. Boy-doggie stew will taste a thousand times better than quadragasserts." Natsy lit a match to the wood; billows of smoke poured upward. "Soon as this water heats up, youse better get ready to be a banquet!"

Percy started to panic, especially after seeing the look on Dilly's face. He sat down on the pit floor. "Don't worry, Dilly," he said, "I'll think of something." Percy dug in his backpack and took out a candle and matchsticks. He mumbled to himself, "I could burn Natsy and we could run away...no, too mean." He rifled through the pack again. Could he shoot the rubber band at Natsy—or throw the bar of soap at him? Would that scare him away? Or how about poking Natsy in the eye with the pencil? Oww!

Percy pulled out the salt and pepper shakers. "Got another idea," he whispered to Dilly. He licked his finger and dipped it into the pepper shaker, then poured a handful of salt into Dilly's paw.

"Natsy," Percy said, standing up on tiptoes, "I think you should believe me when I say we won't make a good meal. We'd taste terrible! How about you sample us first, before you stew us?"

"Fine, I could use a snack. I's so hungry I could eat a live goat!" Natsy leaned over the wall and opened his mouth wide.

Percy stuck his finger inside and felt a pool of spittle, a greasy fang. He rubbed Natsy's tongue with his peppery finger.

Natsy shrieked. "EEEWWW! You're disgusting!" He sneezed and spit. "Harrruuumph! Even a shoe heel can't help you. Let me try the dog."

Percy held Dilly up. Natsy opened his mouth wide again. Dilly stuck his paw in Natsy's mouth and dumped out the mound of salt.

Natsy spewed and slobbered. His tongue swelled. He bolted to the vat, dunked his head in, and drank a gallon of water. "Whew, that was a close call. I's thought I wuz goin' to die from bad taste!" He looked down into the pit. "Youse twos is some kind of spoiled species! Not worth the time it would take to cook ya. I'm leavin'. Gonna find me a little girl. They's full of sugar and spice."

"What about us? You can't leave us here."

"Yes, I can. Maybe someone else will find you eatable."

"I have an idea," Percy said. "If you let us go, I'll give you my sack of food."

"You have food? You've been holding out on me! You *are* a trickster!" Natsy tried to reach into the pit and grab the knapsack, but his arms were too short.

"Help us out of this pit, and the sack is yours," Percy said. "Is that a deal?"

"Toss me the sack, and I'll bring you a ladder," Natsy said.

"Ladder first, then food."

Natsy scrammed and returned with a ladder. He lowered it over the side and waited with open arms. Percy climbed out, holding Dilly. He handed over the sack.

Natsy dumped the food on the ground. "Heewhaaw!" he yelled, jumping up and down. Saliva sprayed everywhere. He attacked the boiled eggs first. Then he tore into the turkey legs, ripped off the meat, and chewed on the bones, one in each hand. "Mmm mmm mmm."

"Can you point us in the right direction?" Percy asked.

Natsy motioned with a bone toward a thicket. He slurped. "Follow the 'Path of Least Resistance.' By the way, what did the gator say to the crockydile?"

Percy grinned as he said, "How come you got all the looks in the family and I look like an old pair of shoes?"

Natsy gagged. Percy and Dilly skeedaddled. When Natsy was out of sight, Percy told Dilly, "I've got good news and bad news. The good news is, without the knapsack I only have to carry the backpack, so the load is lighter. But the bad news is, this is all that's left of our food." He took out two Brussels sprouts pops from his pocket. Dilly's ears drooped. "We'll find something to eat on the mountain. I'm sure of it." Percy hoped that he sounded sure.

They plodded on the "Path of Least Resistance," munching on the pops. Percy told himself not to think about how hungry he was, although he wished he were sitting at the plank table, eating whatever his mom had prepared, with Dilly curled up at his feet.

He tried not to think about what would happen if he and Dilly got so hungry, they had to turn around and go home before they fixed the sun. He tried not to think about how long it would take to die of starvation. But he thought about it anyway.

Thirteen

Fuddy and Duddy

THE PATH HAD BEEN ACCURATELY NAMED—it offered little resistance. Plodding was easy, even going uphill, even being hungry. They traveled far up the mountain. If the rest of the trip proceeded like this, Percy thought, they'd make it to the top in no time.

Unfortunately, the path abruptly ended at a flowered archway. A sign read: "Course of Colors."

"What do you think, Dill? Want to have a look around? Maybe there's something to eat."

Dilly sniffed the air. "Ruff!"

They entered a maze of foliage as tall as Mayor Oscar's newly constructed "His Honor's Office." The walls were covered with ivy, the ground carpeted with a layer of moss. Everything was green and moist. It smelled like springtime after a warm shower.

Dilly scrambled under a green brier and pulled out a worm. He growled, pawing it into a pile of goo.

Percy hurried along. The plants in the maze radiated the brightest green he had ever seen and cast a greenish tint over them. "Hey, Dill, now you really do look like a pickle," Percy said, "good enough to— Look! Food!" Percy found a bush with green apples on it. There were avocados on another, pistachios on another, and olives on another. He ate an apple so fast he almost choked. "Eat up, Dilly!" he sputtered. Percy stuffed food in his mouth as if it were going to disappear any minute. He stuffed even more into his backpack. He felt like Natsy on the loose.

Moving to another group of bushes, Percy first picked off a kiwi and then a green doughy ring. He didn't recognize what kind of food it was, but he bit into it anyway. A donut! It tasted heavenly, even though the color was unsettling. Dilly ate seven in a row.

The Course of Colors wound into a series of turns. Greens faded into whites—a cove dotted with cotton balls and white flowers. Percy recognized honeysuckle, jasmine, and gardenias from his aunt's farm. He sniffed the fragrant air. Dilly sniffed for worms. Percy collected coconut macaroons and white waffles.

They continued through the maze, past walls of golden acacia, to a glade filled with sunflowers and goldenrod. The air glowed bright yellow. Butter biscuits and lemon tarts grew from bushes. Sitting on a giant pineapple, they ate the treats. Percy added more to the growing cache of food in his backpack.

They raced ahead to the next section. A tapestry of pink camellias, geraniums, and begonias swelled through the maze. They stopped in a pasture filled with lollipops, caramels, and gumdrops—all pink! Percy gathered the goodies, and they kept going.

They wound through the maze into a pumpkin patch surrounded by an orchard of miniature tangerine and apricot trees. Orange hibiscus and zinnias were entwined through the trees. Percy stuffed his pockets with fruit.

Moving on, they reached a small clearing where carnations, roses, and cherries grew together. The intense red colored the air a rosy shade.

Percy inhaled. "This place energizes me," he said. "I feel like I could plod forever. And eat forever."

"Ruff."

They followed the maze into a blue grass meadow, bursting with bluebonnets and columbine. A bluish mist hovered over them as they ate blue cheese with blue crackers, which tasted much better than Mrs. Thinley's. In the last section of the maze—a glen covered with lilac, lavender, and violets—the air turned a pale purple shade. Vines loaded with grapes and boysenberry muffins sprouted from the walls. Wisteria spread over the ground. The smell reminded Percy of Auntie Flora's house. He thought she would like this area the best; it was the most peaceful. Percy sighed, patted Dilly's head, and wished Auntie were with them.

Back in Yoosa, Flora visited her sister, Vera, to reassure her about Percy. She brought Vera a bouquet of dried mums and a bow for Peg's tuft of hair.

Vera served romaine tea with endive cookies. Flora remembered that Vera used to make endive cookies when they were children. She had enjoyed cooking with grass.

Vera told Flora she hadn't always noticed Percy when he was there. But since she knew he was gone, she missed him. So did Peg, who crawled into Percy's bedroom every morning looking for him.

"Don't worry so much, Vera," Flora said. "It's not good for your health. Percy will accomplish his goal on the mountain and be back soon. He can handle himself. He's a smart boy."

"He is?" Vera wrinkled her eyebrows. She sipped her tea while Flora fed Peg a bowl of sugar peas. They heard a banging on the front door.

It was five of the six Clumpie Brothers. (Spike had stayed home.) Vera smiled brightly at the boys and invited them inside.

"Howdy, Miss Flora," the boys said in unison. "Need any cottage cheese today?"

"No, thank you," Flora said. "I have dried flower bouquets if you'd like one."

"What would we do with flowers?" Cladam laughed. The other brothers snickered.

Vera held up a pie tin. "How about a piece of pie?"

Clabraham scrutinized it. "Green apple pie, ma'am?"

Clandrew squinted at Peg's bowl, looked stricken. "Pea pie," he muttered.

"No, dears," Vera said. "Green bean pie."

"It's scrumptious," Flora said.

"NO!" The Clumpies turned green while vigorously shaking their heads. Flora watched their heads finally come to a stop, all of them in a cockeyed position.

"I bet you eat your mother's luscious cottage cheese pie," Vera said.

The Clumpies remained green.

"What brings you by?" asked Flora.

Clarthur stepped forward. "We were wondering if you've received any mail from Percy. And if he'd mentioned what weather conditions and land availability were like on Amethyst Mountain. We're fixing to expand our cottage cheese farm, and cottage cheese clots best in cool conditions."

"There's no mail service in Yoosa," Flora said. "The postal farm dried up ages ago."

"It did?"

"Are you sure?"

"That's why we have Dotty Dash."

"Oh," the boys said.

"She transmits the mail with her voice."

"I thought she just stuttered a lot," Clarthur said.

"Maybe too much cottage cheese clots the brain," Flora said.

"I didn't know brains could clot," Clabraham said.

"Remember Mrs. Hydrans?" Claaron said. "Her head swelled up like a milk bucket. They said it could have been giant clots."

"Or maybe giant spiders crawled in her ears," Cladam said.

"Or maybe she got a really, really bad cold, and her head filled up with giant mucous balls!" Clandrew said.

Vera turned green. "Anything else, dears?"

"I can't think of anything," Clabraham said.

"I can believe that," Flora said.

"I guess we should be going."

"Guess or know?" Flora asked.

"Know what?" Claaron looked worried.

"That it's time to go," Flora said.

"How should we know what time it is? Our sundial broke. And we can't figure out how to fix it."

"Maybe you need a watch," Vera said. "Boys, would you like to take broccoli pops home to your parents?"

The Clumpies turned green again. As they left, Peg spit peas at the Clumpie Brothers. The peas ricocheted off the boys' massive backs and rolled around the kitchen floor. Flora thought Percy would be proud of his little sister.

✺ ✺ ✺

Near the end of the Course of Colors, Percy found a batch of wild celery, a deep purple color, growing from the wisteria. He crunched on a stalk and crammed a bunch into his overly-stuffed backpack. "Too bad there wasn't a brown section. I was hoping for steak on a branch. Instead I get celery." He laughed. "I didn't need to travel this far to eat vegetables. I could have stayed home!"

As they exited, a shimmery rainbow hung over them. Percy noticed the rainbow's arch was shaped like Auntie Flora's eyebrows. He couldn't wait to tell her about this extraordinary place.

Beyond the maze, Percy found another path with another sign: "Path of Confusion."

"Oh, boy, Dill, here we go again."

"Ruff!"

Along the way they stopped at a pond. "I hope there aren't any quadragasserts in here," Percy said, filling a cup with water. Dilly gulped from the pond, then dunked his ears in. He shivered.

"Too cold for a bath, Dilly? Valter wouldn't like that."

"R-r-rufff."

They followed the path until it became too dark to continue. They set up camp and dined on olives. Neither was very hungry after gorging themselves earlier. Soon they were asleep, curled up together to keep warm, and so tired that they forgot to remove their glasses.

On the morning of the fifth day, Percy discovered the path split in two directions. A sign read: "Follow My Way." An arrow pointed to the left with the word "West" painted beneath it. Another arrow pointed to the right with the word "East" below it.

Percy frowned. "This is not a good sign, Dilly," he said. "How can I make the right choice? I don't even know which way we should go, except up."

High-pitched laughter rang out from behind the sign. Two odd-looking boys popped out, bouncing from side to side. Bowl haircuts framed their large round heads. They had floppy arms and broomstick legs in striped stockings. Each had a pinwheel belly that spun in circles—one was green and yellow, the other red and orange. They looked exactly alike, except one wore a knit cap, and the other wore a beanie. The one with the beanie smacked the other one on the head.

"Ow, *that* hurts," said the one in the knit cap.

The one in the beanie hit the other one on the shoulder. "No, *that* hurts."

"No, that hurts," said the other one as he kicked the beanied one in the leg.

Percy grimaced. "Ooww."

The twosome turned at the same time toward Percy. "Ikkugg!" they said together. Their bellies spun around like tops, one clockwise, the other counterclockwise.

"What is it?" said one.

"Can't tell," said the other.

"An intruder."

"An ijit?"

"Can't tell."

"Are its shoelaces tied together?"

"No."

"Shirt on backwards?"

"No."

"Hair stick straight up?"

"Yes."

"Ah, possibly an ijit."

"Excuse me. I'm Percy, a *boy,* from Yoosa."

"Interesting," said the one with the beanie.

"What's an ijit?" Percy asked.

"If you weren't one, you'd know."

"They never know. Does a doofus, or an ignoramus?"

"Maybe a numbskull. But never an ijit."

Percy was puzzled. What were they talking about?

One gestured his arm at Dilly. "And is that your pet pickle?"

Dilly growled.

The twosome giggled.

"No, that's my *dog,* Dilly."

"Ikkugg on him," said the one in the beanie. "I'm Dud."

"I'm Fud," said the other. "Ever heard of us?"

"I know what a dud is," Percy said, "but I've never heard of a fud."

"See, Fuddy, I told you I was more famous than you," Dud said.

"Are not, Duddy," Fud said.

"Am, too." Dud smacked Fud on the arm.

"Ow, that hurts!"

"No, *that* hurts." Another smack.

"Stop that!" yelled Percy. "It's not nice to hit each other."

"Ikkugg!" Fuddy said. "Who wants to be nice?" His belly spun around.

"Are you related to the Malatete Twins?" Percy asked.

"Twins, ha! We're clones."

"Clones of what?"

"An experiment."

"What kind of experiment?"

"A social-political-economical kind."

"A comical cosmical kind."

What were they talking about? Percy rubbed his head. Dilly slumped on the ground.

"What do you do?" asked Fuddy.

"Right now I'm on a journey to the top of Amethyst Mountain," Percy said.

Fud and Dud tittered loudly, bouncing from side to side.

"And what is it that you do?" Percy asked, irritation in his voice.

"We confuse," Duddy said.

"We muddle," Fuddy said.

"We bewilder."

"We discombobulate."

"I'm perplexed," Percy said.

"Now you've got it."

"Why do you want to confuse?"

"Gratification."

"What life is all about, don't you think?"

"I'm not sure what you mean," Percy said. "But I don't have time for philosophy or quarreling or confusion. I need to get to the top of the mountain right away. Can you please tell me, which way is the fastest?"

"My way, of course," Duddy said, pointing east.

"No, my way," Fuddy said, pointing west.

"My way," they said, flapping their arms in different directions. "My way, my way, my way...."

Percy's ears buzzed. He put his hands over them, trying to think. If these two were trying to confuse, then going either west or east would be confusing, wouldn't it? East or west would muddle him, wouldn't it? Or would it perplex him? He walked straight ahead, proceeding north.

"Where do you think you're going?" Fuddy's pinwheel belly spun into a blur of yellowish green.

"You're heading straight into Grizzman territory!" Duddy's belly whirled into a blur of reddish orange.

"YOU'RE AN IJIT!" they screeched.

Ikkugg on them! Percy ventured ahead, path or no path, Dilly right behind. He heard Fuddy's (or was it Duddy's?) high-pitched voice in the distance, "You'll be soooorry."

"Dill, I don't care if we are going the wrong way, as long as it's away from them! They're a double headache. We'll get to the top—eventually."

Dilly didn't respond. Was he worried? Did he sense danger? Percy wondered what Dilly thought about their adventure so far. Was it a good idea? Should they have stayed home? Was he putting Dilly in jeopardy as Droll had said he was?

Percy gazed at the sun. What used to be a bright pie lighting up the countryside was now a crumb in a gray smeary sky. They had to keep going. So up they plodded the entire day, until finally....

Fourteen

Luster Krupter

BOBBYDAZZLER!" FOR THE FIRST TIME, Percy could see the summit of Amethyst Mountain. "Look, Dill, we're almost there! Can you believe it? Plodding works!"

"RUFF!"

They stopped for the night at a barren plateau. Percy shook out the blankets and spread them on the ground. He counted out blueberries and divided a lemon tart for dinner. The frosty air cut through his sweater. He didn't say anything to Dilly about the cold. He thought he heard strange noises, like cackling and honking, but he didn't mention that either. They huddled together as Percy read aloud from his book. He felt a warm wind blow over them. It boosted his confidence. "Tomorrow is a big day, Dilly. We'll be able to rope the sun back in."

Dilly rolled over on his back and snorted.

Percy thought back over the last several days. His stomach flipped and flopped. They were so close to accomplishing their goal. Nothing could go wrong now, could it?

Back in Yoosa, people had decided they needed a different solution to fix the sun problem—other than one which involved Percy Veerance. Spurred on by desperation, many Yoosians offered ideas. Mr. Sushiyama suggested throwing a fishing net over the sun as it set for the evening and wasn't looking. Vic Brickhauser bragged he could build a brick staircase to the sun—probably within three to four years. Mrs. Mortimer said that an invitation to an elegant luncheon could persuade the sun to make a noontime appearance. Bronco Snozhead swore bribes worked. But Yoosians liked Icabod Tubula's idea best: building a robot and sending it up in a hot air balloon to rope the sun back in.

"There's not enough hot air in Yoosa anymore to fill up the balloon."

"The mayor is full of it."

It didn't matter. The robot idea didn't work out. Yoosians argued who should build which part and what material to use ("Iron," Mr. Borden said; "Pig skin," Mr. Malatete said; "Clay," Mr. Hohokam said.) They bickered over what it should look like ("a banana," "a hair curler," "a flute") and quibbled over the color of the balloon (every color but chartreuse was mentioned).

"Lack of sunlight has pickled your brains," Rocky Cardia said.

"Where are pickles?" Mrs. Tubula said.

They couldn't even agree on a name. Mrs. Id suggested "The Flying Sequin;" Bard suggested "Hither and Yon into the Yonder;" Mr. Kismet suggested "Nit Picked." They were all booed. The Malatete Twins threw sticks and stones.

Ursula Fellini offered her cat in lieu of a robot. "Pookins can pull the string and bring the sun back in," she said. Snide remarks abounded, especially about brain cells. Rocky Cardia said Miss Fellini's idea was a good one. Then he proposed ejecting Pookins from the balloon at two thousand feet to see if it would land on its feet. Miss Fellini burst into tears. Linus was the quickest to offer a hankie.

People's moods mirrored the ugly sky. They fretted themselves into despair, ill health, weight gain, and hair loss. The mayor set up an advisory committee to nominate more solutions to the sun problem. But Yoosians couldn't agree where to meet.

For Percy, another gray and gloomy morning announced the beginning of day number six. But nothing could dampen his spirits. He was too close to fixing the sun! Trudging across the plateau, he and Dilly came upon another sign: "Stairs to Shiny Shrine."

"I bet that's where the sun is roped," Percy said. The stairway traversed upward to the mountain peak. Percy and Dilly ascended the hundreds and hundreds of steps.

The stairway ended in a courtyard made of hardened lava. Jagged cracks crisscrossed the area. Chunks of crimson and black volcanic rocks protruded from the ground, which was covered with burnt sod and swirls of orange grit. It smelled like ashes.

The courtyard was encircled by dozens of porcelain statues. Percy noticed they all looked the same: a seven-foot-high man with a handsome face, wearing a crown, holding a torch.

In the middle of the courtyard, a fountain squirted fire. Pale yellow flames leapt into the sky and crackled like popping corn. Across from it, Shiny Shrine jutted from the ground like a glistening volcano. It was dome-shaped and covered in a mosaic of shiny metal tiles. Topaz-colored flames cascaded from a minaret on the roof. The flames reflected onto the tiles, making the shrine look as if it were blazing with fire.

Percy shivered. Even with all the fire around him, there was no warmth. He was curious to see inside, see how the sun was roped into the shrine. He proceeded slowly through the vaulted doorway, Dilly following one step behind. Inside, Percy scanned the area. No sign of a rope. But Shiny Shrine was the most spectacular building he'd ever seen. It had a gilded ceiling and copper floor. The tiled walls were decorated with bronze shields and beveled mirrors. Torches burned brightly. An iridescent stage, made of silver and opals, glimmered in the far end of the room. Around it were swords and lances of all sizes, handles encrusted with emeralds, stuck in the floor like a forbidding picket fence. Centered in the stage was a golden throne speckled with diamonds.

Firelight from the torches reflected off the ceiling, floor, shields, mirrors, swords, stage, and throne and bounced around the room like a fireworks display. Percy wished he were wearing sunglasses, but he was too entranced by the display to dig them out of his backpack. Dilly crouched and squinted.

But the most fascinating thing of all was the figure who sat on the throne—a life-sized version of the statues outside—a real man with a perfect face, as if sculpted by an artist. His eyes were like hematite crystals; his slicked-back hair shone like obsidian. A platinum crown with six spires rested on his head. He wore a sapphire choker and a long glittery robe of purple and silver. His shoulders were enormous, his arms thick. When he smiled, the rubies in his teeth twinkled. His ivory fingernails gleamed.

Spellbound, Percy gaped at the man who looked like a lustrous king. But Dilly charged at him, grabbing the hem of his coat and pulling.

"Stop it, Dilly!"

The beautiful, shiny man smacked Dilly with his scepter. "It's not polite to pull on people's clothes. Being rude will get you into deep doo-doo. A prodigious bird once told me that."

The man sparkled so much, Percy felt queasy. He had to avert his eyes from time to time. Dilly knelt on his haunches, paws over his eyes.

"Welcome to my temple," the shiny man said." My name is Luster Krupter."

Percy wondered if it hurt to talk with rubies in your teeth. He'd have to ask Mr. Dent.

"Although some people call me Larcenous Lardy-Dardy."

Percy didn't know what that meant, but he felt his cowlick spring up. "That's an interesting name," he said.

"I rather enjoy it."

"Are you royalty?"

"Not at the moment."

"But you're wearing a crown."

"I'm practicing."

Percy stared.

"What are you staring at?"

"You're—you're really beautiful—in a kind of unusual way."

"Thank you, kid."

"How did you get the rubies in your teeth?"

"I hammered them in."

Percy cringed. "Didn't that hurt?"

"One must suffer for one's vanity. You're very inquisitive. What's your name?"

"I'm Percy from Yoosa. You sure have a shiny place. We don't have anything like it in Yoosa."

"Call it the Luster touch. And is that a round worm you brought with you?"

Dilly looked up, growled, then quickly lowered his head.

"He's my dog, Dilly."

"Looks like a worm with stumps." Luster cackled, a rascally laugh. "And I ought to know."

"Luster, why do you have so many statues of yourself?"

"To remind myself how good-looking I am."

Percy scrunched up his face.

"Vanity, vanity. It's all vanity, kid!"

Percy asked, "Does your family live here?"

"No. No family, no friends, or anyone else. I don't need people when I'm surrounded by riches. And what good are riches if you don't show them off?"

Percy thought, *If you have friends instead of jewels, you don't have to keep company with statues.* (Sounded like a Floraism!)

"What brings you to my humble temple?"

"I'm looking for the rope to the sun. "

Luster gritted his teeth. "What the blazing beejeebies for?" His teeth sparkled like red light beams that shot through Percy's glasses, blinding him.

Percy turned his head and said, "I need to pull the sun back to Yoosa."

Luster sneered. "A kid like you is no match for the sun. But now I'm curious. What makes you think you can rope the sun back in?"

"I can plod."

Luster laughed a haughty laugh. It unnerved Percy. "You're quite amusing for a kid," Luster said. "But the rope isn't here."

"But isn't this the top of the mountain?"

"No, this is a false summit."

"Oh. Do you know where the rope is?"

"Yes."

"Can you take me there?"

"It's a taxing journey to the top. Up another flight of stairs, the Stoney Steps, very steep. Why don't you rest, and we'll go later?"

"I want to go now."

"I'm busy."

"Doing what?"

"Being prideful."

"Can't you do that later? Please, Luster?"

Luster emitted a razzle-dazzle smile. Percy decided that regular teeth were better.

"Very well. I'll show you the location. But your dog must stay." An unpleasant tone had seeped into Luster's voice.

Dilly's ears shot straight up.

"Why?"

"Too precipitous. The dog is too short. He waits for you or we don't go."

"Is that all right, Dilly?"

Dilly dashed toward Luster, who shoved the scepter in his face again. "Blazing beejeebies!"

Percy retrieved his dog. "Sorry, I don't know what's gotten into him. He usually likes everybody."

"Secure him by the fountain. I don't want him scratching my weapons, or for blazing sakes, piddling on anything!" He went out the vaulted door—moving in a strange, almost undulating way.

Percy put Dilly next to the fountain. "Stay here and keep an eye on my backpack." He gave Dilly a peck on the snout. "I'll be back soon, I promise." Dilly's ears stuck straight up.

At the far edge of the courtyard, Luster stood near a cluster of thornbushes sculpted into a topiary Luster statue. Percy thought there were red berries on the branches. But they weren't berries. They were red eyes belonging to green spiders the size of field mice! With suckers on the ends of their eight legs! Percy held back a scream.

"You like them? They're Biter Spiders," Luster said. "I bred them myself—part octopus, part tarantula. They guard my secret passageway to the mountain peak. They won't hurt you—unless I tell them to." A sinister look appeared on Luster's face. "Then they'll suck the life right out of you!" He tickled one of the spiders. It waved its sucker. "See, they're friendly. You must go through the spiders to reach the steps."

Luster reached through the spiders and gripped a handle. He swung the thorny gate aside, exposing the Stoney Steps. "To the top!" Luster commanded, then slithered away.

Percy struggled to keep pace with Luster. The steps were hard and cold. He reached down to touch them—icy. Luster slinked farther ahead. Percy moved more slowly. His toes were frozen.

"Aren't the stairs cold on your feet?" Percy called out.

"No, I'm cold-blooded," Luster said.

The stairway wove back and forth up a severe incline. As they climbed higher, the air became thinner and colder. Percy huffed and puffed. "This is the crookedest path I've ever been on."

"Thank you," Luster said. "I designed it myself."

At the top, Percy beheld another amazing sight—a boulder the size of his Grandpap's cricket compound. It partially concealed an underground tunnel where a silver rope, as big around as a barrel, extended from it. Miles of the rope coiled on the ground like a gargantuan metallic snake.

This was the rope attached to the sun! He'd made it! "Who moved the boulder and pulled the rope out of the ground?" Percy asked.

"Who knows? Could be a naturally occurring geologic condition, like my beauty.""

Percy strained to pick up the rope. It was impossibly heavy. "Luster, can you help me?"

"As I said before, you are no match for the sun. It would take more than two of us to pull it in."

"But who else is there?"

"Geese."

"Birds?!"

"They're strong and numerous."

"Can you ask them to help us?"

"No!"

"Why not?"

"Because...because..." Luster stammered, "because they're away—on vacation. I showed you the rope's location. That's it for today."

Luster darted down the icy steps. Percy followed, slipping and sliding partway, so frozen he didn't feel the bumps and bruises. At the bottom of the stairs, he ran through the thorny gate without looking at the spiders and into the courtyard to the fountain of fire. His backpack was exactly where he'd left it—but Dilly was not. "Dilly? Where are you, boy?" No Dilly. Percy called out over and over as he searched the entire courtyard: behind the Luster statues, in the shrine, around the stage.

Luster sat on his throne with a bemused look on his face. "Don't think your mutt is in here, kid."

"DILLY!" Percy clapped his hands and whistled. "Luster," he said, "Dilly's gone! Where could he be?"

"I have no idea."

"Did the spiders get him?"

"Don't be absurd. I wasn't here to give the command."

Percy felt as if he had been kicked in the stomach by Stanley (Mr. Snozhead's stallion). "Where, oh where, has my little dog gone?" he cried.

"Control yourself, kid. Maybe he ran away."

"Dilly would never do that. He always minds me." Percy gulped. His eyes bulged with fear. "I think Dilly's been stolen!"

"Yes, that's it, probably," Luster said. "You have heard about Grizzman, haven't you? He must have your dog. No one else on the mountain could be as cunning. If you want your dog back, you must find Grizzman and smite him! I'll loan you one of my swords." Luster pulled a sword from the floor and flung it in the air.

Percy caught the sword by the emerald handle. The weight of it strained his arm. "You mean, slay him?"

"Behead, disembowel, amputate his heart—whatever it takes," Luster said. "You have no choice. And you better hope you're not too late."

Percy felt ill. "How do I find Grizzman?"

"Follow Skyward Path, behind the shrine."

Not another path....

Percy plodded along Skyward Path—which was not made for look-ing up. Instead, he had to constantly look down—to avoid stumbling into potholes. He renamed the path: "Trail To A Void." The one good thing about potholes: they distracted Percy from his crushing emo-tions. Sometimes sadness pierced his heart; sometimes fear shook his bones; sometimes anger filled his body. But mostly he felt disgust at himself for losing Dilly.

Percy plodded, whacked flying insects with the sword, and stabbed at the potholes with a vengeance. On and on. *Keep going. Rescue Dilly. But kill Grizzman?* Percy shuddered. He flung the sword into the woods. There had to be a better way. He hoped that whatever it was, it would miraculously come to him when he found Grizzman.

The path seemed to lead nowhere. Had Luster given him the wrong directions? The dismal sky made Percy feel worse—worse even than when Biff Stuffy had stuffed him into the coat closet at school and locked him in all night, and his parents hadn't noticed he was missing. Worse than the time he won the Library Award, and his dad told him he should put more effort into picking vegetables.

But now Dilly was gone. Nothing could be worse than that! Was he still alive? How could Percy find him? He plodded until he couldn't go another inch. He had to stop for the night.

He rubbed his stomach. In a hurry to leave Shiny Shrine, he had left his backpack by the fountain. That meant no dinner, no blanket, no book to take his mind off his troubles. He sat on the ground, clasp-ing his knees to his chest. He imagined a king-size chicken potpie with a thick crust and creamy gravy. He pretended to smell the steamy aroma. He pretended to stick a fork in the pie and take a bite. He imagined each mouth-watering bite. After a while, his stomach felt full. He curled up in the dirt, looking up at the sky. No stars to make a wish, but he wished anyway—for someone to help him find Dilly. And someone to confront Grizzman for him.

An opaque moon blinked down at him. "Why didn't you drift away, Mr. Moon, instead of the sun? Then I wouldn't be in this mess."

As Percy fell asleep, he heard Auntie Flora's dreamy voice, "If you need help, find Ima. She lives next to Zeal Crater."

Fifteen

Ima N. Thused

ON DAY NUMBER SEVEN, Percy needed answers: how was he going to get Dilly back? Should he seek help from Ima? Did he have time to go down the mountain to Zeal Crater instead of up to find Grizzman? *Make a decision! Okay, no time for breakfast.* (No food, anyway.) This was the time to find a better route than Skyward Path. Maybe Ima knew one.

Percy plodded down the mountain. Pulling his sweater around him, he thought of garbanzo bean porridge, and of dipping his hands in it to keep warm. He even thought of eating it. But mostly he thought about rescuing Dilly.

Percy reached a precipice. Below, dense woodlands sloped into a valley. "How am I going to find a crater in that thick forest?"

Just then, as with the tumbleweed blockade, a strong wind blew past and gushed through the forest, separating trees like a crowd of people stepping aside for a royal procession. Through the parted branches, Percy saw a mammoth hole in the earth, like a carved bowl, twice the size of Dreary Lake and Cheery Lake combined. Must be Zeal Crater!

He had to hurry. Plodding had become too slow; it required too much patience. It was time for faster transportation. Percy got an idea. He scavenged a piece of tree bark as big as he was. He flattened it with a stone, then folded up the edges to fashion a sled. He sat on the sled and pushed off with a stick. Down the mountain he slid, swerving between trees, swinging the stick from side to side like paddling a kayak. He picked up speed. His hair flew up as he flew past flying birds. His face stretched back; his glasses embedded into his forehead.

Percy maneuvered deftly around trees and boulders. He began to feel like an invincible knight on a crusade galloping through a battlefield! But the faster he went, the harder it was to guide the sled. He skimmed over rocks and twigs. Ouch! He bumped up and down like a roller coaster. Ow ow ow! He grazed tree stumps. Ouch! So fast that friction caused the sled to heat up. Owww!

Percy zoomed too close to a pine tree. He tried to push away from it, but his stick snapped in two. Part of the sled ripped off. Whoooah! He lost control and careened downhill. Faster and faster he skidded, through the forest and into the valley.

Here comes the crater! How am I going to stop? Percy's final thought: *Where did that maple tree come from?* He covered his eyes. Whack! Sap! He smacked headfirst into the tree trunk and propelled out of the sled like a human cannonball. He rotated twice in the air and landed on his back beneath the tree. Maple syrup dripped on his head. But he didn't feel a thing—he'd been knocked unconscious.

All day Percy lay in a supine position. Birds flew overhead and wondered what the boy was doing sprawled there on the ground. A swarm of bees harvested the syrup from Percy's face. A roving gang of youthful elfoons happened by. One elfoon picked his pocket and ate the lint. One poked at him with a fork and knife, but decided that Percy was too cold and dead to eat. Another tried to steal his glasses until a spear whizzed past the elfoon's head. The gang ran away.

Darkness settled over the area like a black cloth. Percy would have frozen to death had a warm wind not blown over him all night.

He awakened, quivering. The air was sharp, the sun reduced to a red dot, like one of the Biter Spider's eyes, barely able to cast light into the sky. Percy was so thirsty that it hurt to swallow. How long had he been out? Was today day eight? Had he wasted a whole day flat on his back when Dilly was still missing? His head pounded. He felt a lump. "Oww!" He remembered where he'd been going. He sat up and groaned. His body felt as if it had recently crashed into a tree.

But at least he had found Zeal Crater. It looked like a deep dish of silvery powder. Percy would have liked to run through it, but he was low on energy and time, and he needed to find Ima. There was only one house within sight. It had honeycomb walls and roof and a wraparound verandah. Walking toward it, he saw a golden door with an apple design. Flower gardens surrounded the house. A sign planted in the yard confirmed what Percy had guessed: "Home of Ima N. Thused."

He took a deep breath before knocking on the door. A grandmotherly woman opened it. She had white hair twisted into a bun. Freckles on her lined face flickered like fireflies. A lacy shawl covered her shoulders. Pink glasses perched on her nose.

"Who's there?" the woman asked cheerfully.

"Percy."

"You smell like a maple tree, Percy."

"I've been sleeping in the forest."

"Not such a good place, I suspect." She laughed. The skin on her cheeks jiggled.

"It wasn't my idea."

"You have a nice voice, Percy. Have you come here to visit me?"

"Are you Miss Ima Thused?"

She nodded. "Ima all my life, so call me that."

"Ima, my Aunt Flora told me to find you."

"Oh, my stars, one of Flora's relatives? How exciting!" She flung her arms wide. "Welcome. Come in!" She opened the door and stepped aside. She felt for the doorknob and closed the door behind her. "Have a seat over there." Ima pointed to a tall chest.

Percy chose a divan instead and sank into white fluffy cushions. He glanced around the room. The wood-burning stove was not lit, but should have been because the room was so chilly. Children's drawings done with colored pencils hung on the walls. He saw another room that was filled with books stacked clear to the ceiling. Hundreds of them, dusty and old.

On the chest, he spied a portrait of a young girl. Her hair was gold-streaked, tied up in a bun with a blue ribbon. In her hands was a bride doll and a teacup. "Is that you in the painting?" Percy asked.

"Oh, no," Ima said. "That painting is much older than I. That's my grandmother. People say I look like her. Would you care for a cup of tea?"

"I would be grateful!"

"There's water in the kettle. And the cups are...somewhere..."

"I'll find them," Percy said. He retrieved them from a shelf, then lit the stove.

"Tell me how your aunt is doing."

"Good, except for the sun problem."

"What's wrong with the sun?" asked Ima, not looking at Percy.

"It's drifting away. Sunlight is fading more each day. Hadn't you noticed?"

"I wondered why it was so cold this summer."

Percy stared at Ima's eyes. They twinkled with gold flecks but didn't focus. "I hope you don't mind me asking, Ima, but are you blind?"

"More or less. I'm able to see shapes, but not details."

"Why do you plant flowers if you can't see them?"

"I can smell them, I can feel them, I can eat them."

Eat them! Was Ima serious?

"What is not seen is more important than what can be seen."

What did that mean? Percy would have to ask his aunt. "Where did you get all the honeycombs to build your house?"

"Honey Tears Gulch."

No wonder there wasn't any honey there. "Why do you have so many books?"

"I started collecting them as a child."

"So you weren't born blind?"

"I lost my sight when I was a girl."

"What happened?"

"It's silly, really, not much of a story."

"I love stories."

"Perhaps I'll tell you someday."

The teakettle whistled. Percy poured bubbly water into cups with tea leaves. He handed a cup to Ima. He blew on the tea and drank it as fast as he could, then poured a second cup. The tea warmed Percy's bones, relaxed him. He sank back into the divan. "Do you get lonely here by yourself, Ima?"

"I'm not alone. I have nature all around me. And Numen."

"Who's Numen?"

"My helper. He cooks and cleans, prepares meals, reads to me. He's a very talented dodo."

"A real dodo? I thought they were extinct. I read that in a book."

"Can't believe everything you read, Percy. Dodos don't like to bring attention to themselves, but they're around. And they make wonderful companions. They're caring, encouraging. Plus, very charming." She smiled. "People should be more dodo-ish."

"But they're dumb."

"On the contrary, they're quite intelligent."

Percy would like to see for himself. "Where is Numen?"

"On a chirp talk mission. He's been gone for weeks, visiting magpie families. They get so glum. If anyone can cheer them up, it's Numen. I'd love to introduce you to him so you can make up your own mind. Then if anybody ever calls you a dodo, you can take it as a compliment!"

The conflicting information about dodos made Percy think of something else. "Ima, do you know how Stinko Swamp got its bad smell?"

"It's a natural geologic phenomenon," she said. "Heavy rains cause sulfur residues to drain off the P.U. Plain and deposit into the swamp."

"That's it? No fable or myth?"

"No."

"No funny yarn?"

"No."

"No B.O. Corpus? No rotten eggs? No quadragasserts?"

"Heavens, no. The smell in Stinko Swamp is part of the natural order of odors." Ima chuckled.

"Oh," Percy said, disappointed that the stories he'd heard weren't true.

"Percy, how about something to eat?"

"Yes, please!" (He thought she'd never ask, famished as he was.)

Ima set a bowl on the table filled with seeds, flowers, plants, and fungi. "Help yourself."

Percy stared into the bowl. Nobody could eat that stuff. "I don't mean to be rude, Ima, but maybe you didn't put out the right bowl of food?"

"I'm so embarrassed!" She laughed. "Did I give you Numen's meal?" She felt everything in the bowl, then made a funny face. "Percy, this is food for you."

"It is? But it's a bouquet of flowers!"

"I know, nasturtiums and violas. Quite edible. Quite good. And so are the caraway seeds, fiddle fern, and truffles."

Where was his mom's cooking when he needed it? "I'll try the seeds," Percy said.

"Caraway seeds are my favorite. You can eat them. And fling a handful in the air and say, 'Cares, go away!' Never underestimate the power of a seed."

Percy ate a few seeds. They were crunchy, nutty. Not bad tasting.

"Try the fiddle fern. You'll love it."

Percy took a small bite. It tasted like a combination of lettuce and Mrs. Thinley's paper crackers.

"Now, the flowers."

"I'll take them with me, in case I get hungry later."

"Good idea. Put them in one of my totebags. And some watercress, too, in case you get thirsty. And how about the truffles?"

"No, thanks. I think I'm allergic to mold."

Ima laughed. "I have some almonds, kumquats, and chocolate-covered cherries you can take. You're a growing boy. I hear it in your bones. By the way, Percy, you haven't told me what brought you to the mountain."

"The sun problem. To fix it so we can have regular sunshine again in Yoosa. My dog Dilly and I—" Percy had been so interested in Ima and food and drink and stories, he'd forgotten the reason he'd come to her house: DILLY! He choked on a piece of fern. "I lost my dog! And it's all my fault! I let him get stolen, and now I have to rescue him at the top of the mountain before it's too late!" Percy started to cry. "I lost my best friend," he blubbered, wiping his nose on his sleeve. "I should never have come to the mountain. People told me I didn't have what it takes, but I didn't listen. They were right. How could I be so dumb!?"

"Take a deep breath, Percy, and hold it. Now exhale." Ima lifted her hands up as Percy inhaled, then lowered them as he exhaled. She conducted Percy's breathing as she talked. "Feel better? Good. Setting out to accomplish something is not dumb, Percy. It's admirable. You've had a setback. Nothing terminal. When you run into roadblocks, do what I do: circumambulate."

Percy exhaled. "Circum—what?"

"Cir-cum-am-bu-late the roadblocks. Go around them."

Percy sniffled. "My aunt said you'd help me." But how could an old blind lady who lived with a dodo help him?

"What you need are good directions and a good attitude. Try optimism. It's a force multiplier. And expect the best to happen."

"But how can I when I'm worried about Grizzman?"

Ima continued conducting. "Barry Grizzman is a mystery, but he's nothing to worry about. I've never met him face-to-face, but I know who he is. He's inhabited these slopes as long as I've been here, and peacefully, too. Sometimes when I'm strolling through the Course of

Colors, I can smell him. I call out 'Who's there?' but he doesn't answer. Other times, I hear him in the rustle of trees, or sense him ambling through my flower gardens."

"I think Grizzman stole Dilly! And everyone says he's a monster!"

"That's not true, Percy. He's no monster. He's shy. And he smells sweet. If Grizzman has your dog, he won't harm him. He used to have a pet wolf, and that wolf meant everything to him."

"I feel that way about Dilly. I wish you could see him, Ima...I mean meet him. He's the best." Percy swallowed to ease the lump in his throat and took a deep breath as Ima lifted her arms up.

"When you find Dilly, I'd love to meet him. In the meantime, keep an open mind about Grizzman. Things aren't always as they appear to be. As for you, take the totebag of food and focus on the present task at hand. Your breathing sounds good now." She rested her arms. "Hike up the left side of the mountain. Look for a sign that says 'Zenith Path.' Stay to the left, not the right, because that will lead you to Shiny Shrine, a place to avoid. And one more thing before you go. Try these on..." Ima gave Percy a pair of boots made from woven leaves, the laces made from ivy vines. Attached to the soles was a rubber plant stalk wound into a spiral. "I call them 'Tude Boots. I wear them hiking around the mountain. At my age, I need all the extra spring I can get!" She laughed.

"Will they help me plod?"

"They're plod boosters."

Percy slipped the boots over his tattered shoes and tied the laces around his ankles. He took one step and sprung up high. He hopped around the room. "Bobbydazzler! You should see me, Ima. I've got optimism in my feet!" Carrying the totebag, he bounced out the door. "Thanks, Ima. You've been a big help!"

Ima blew kisses in Percy's general direction.

With each plod, Percy sprang two feet from the ground. He felt as if he'd taken a dose of Auntie Flora's H.O.P. powder. He quickly made it out of the valley and found Zenith Path. As he bounced along, he shouted to the sky, "Oh where, oh where has my little dog gone?"

Sixteen

🎵 Confronting Grizzman

ITH ONE FINAL BOUNCE, Percy landed atop Amethyst Mountain. He'd made it! He pulled off the 'Tude Boots and stashed them with the totebag behind a mulberry bush. A line of redwood trees circled what he presumed was Grizzman's cabin. Behind the trees was a windmill surrounded by a small orchard of almond and walnut trees.

The cabin leaned to one side and the door hung on rusted hinges. The faded black roof dipped in the middle, reminding Percy of Mona. The deteriorated condition reminded him of Mrs. Mortimer's chicken coop. The ashen shade of the walls could have been a new classification color for the Pettifog Fogies—"Grizzman cabin gray." If Grizzman was as huge as everyone said he was—and Percy hoped he wasn't—the house looked too small for him.

Birdhouses of all sizes were draped from the eves like ornaments. Feeding dishes were scattered throughout the yard. A kitten licked milk from a bowl. A cow licked a salt brick. It didn't look as if anyone scary lived there.

"Dilly, where are you?" Percy called out. "Come here, boy!" He whistled, clapped his hands. "I've come to get you," he said, his voice cracking. The cow mooed and the kitten ran away. Percy kept calling. He waited for Dilly to come bounding at him. No Dilly.

Percy pounded on the lopsided door. "Grizzman, are you in there? I want my dog back!" He waited. No answer.

This was no time to be pole-ite. Percy opened the door, wide enough to stick his head inside. "I'm here, Dilly. Come on, boy!" No response.

Percy opened the door wider and stepped inside. His feet squeaked on the wooden floor. He perused the place. Grizzman's cabin was one room, kept clean and orderly. A table fit against each wall. One was stacked with nuts and fruit. Another displayed carved wooden figures of animals. The third table held a pretty ceramic dish and a bell. On the fourth table were objects he'd never seen before: clear glass orbs with wires inside.

Percy felt funny being in a stranger's house alone. He went outside and began calling for Dilly and Grizzman again.

A creature disguised in a bear rug, head, and claws jumped out from behind a tree, began pouncing on all fours. Percy's cowlick flew up, then settled down. The creature growled like a bear but hopped like a frog.

"Mr. Bear, have you seen Grizzman?" Percy said. "I want to get my dog back."

The bear-creature growled again.

This was not a scary creature, Percy thought, more like *odd*. And it wore leather shoes! Percy grinned. "I know it's you, Grizzman. Take off that costume. I'm Percy Veerance from Yoosa."

Grizzman stood up. "I used to live there," he said.

"I know."

"How do you know about me?" Grizzman asked in a quiet voice, removing the bear-rug cape.

When Grizzman removed the bear head, Percy almost jumped out of his skin. What a galoot! Grizzman was scarier than a bear! His whole face was like the rough part of Droll Troll. But he was bigger. Percy caught his breath. "You're a legend in Yoosa."

"Tell me, Percy. Do Yoosians still think I'm a monster?"

Percy gulped. "Well...sort of..."

"I thought so. Some things never change. What are you doing here?"

"I've come to get my dog."

"What dog?"

"Dilly. He looks like a fuzzy brown cucumber, but he doesn't have a tail."

"I haven't seen him," Grizzman said.

"Yes, you have, because you stole him! And you have to give him back!"

"I don't steal pets."

Percy felt a twinge in his stomach. It was unnerving to look at Grizzman. "Luster told me you did."

"What?! He's wrong. I'd never do that." Grizzman looked sad. "You must believe me. Your dog's not here."

"Listen, Big Hairy Barry Grizzman!" Percy stepped closer. "I've faced Stinko Swamp, a troll, Fuddy and Duddy, Natsy Gnat, treacherous terrain, bad weather, starvation, and crashing into a tree. I've had enough of this mountain, so give me my dog back! I want to go home!" Percy lunged toward Grizzman, who blew a warm breeze at Percy, suspending him in stop-motion. Percy swung his arms and rotated his legs, but got nowhere. He hollered, "Let me go!"

Grizzman stopped blowing. "Animals are my friends," he said. "I would never hurt a dog."

"Then where's Dilly?"

"My guess...the *real* monster of the mountain has him."

"Who's that?"

"Luster Krupter."

"Luster? He's no monster, he's nice."

"You're not looking beneath the surface."

"He said he'd help me rope the sun back in."

"He has no intention of doing that. Luster is the enemy of sunlight."

"He told me he'd get a family of geese to help me."

"The geese are his army. He's trained them. Every day they pull the rope to the sun further out of the underground tunnel, which is why the sun keeps moving farther away."

Percy scrunched up his face. "How do you know that?"

"I've watched them, for almost a year. And when I could, I blew the geese away."

"Why would Luster do that? He knows we need the sun."

"Luster controls fire. If there is no sun, then he controls the only access to heat and light. And people would be at his mercy."

Percy didn't want to believe it. "You're lying."

"That's Luster's way, not mine."

"Why should I believe you?"

"Because I don't have your dog. Look for yourself, then decide."

Percy knew that if Dilly were around, he would have let Percy know by now.

"Go back to Shiny Shrine," Grizzman said. "That's where you'll find your dog."

It was hard to believe Grizzman. "If what you say is true, then what Luster's doing is terrible. How could someone so beautiful be so awful?"

"Things aren't always as they appear to be."

Percy thought for a minute. "Do you know what a larcenous lardy-dardy is?"

"It's someone who lies to you and takes something valuable from you without your consent."

Percy wailed, "How could I let this happen to Dilly?!"

Grizzman reached out to put his hand on Percy's shoulder. Percy shrugged away. He saw the hurt look on Grizzman's face.

"I'm afraid Luster needs to get rid of you and your dog," Grizzman said, "because you're spoiling his plans. If you'd like, I can help you—"

"No, I'm on my own." Percy eyed Grizzman, who looked sincere, but in a frightening sort of way. Percy couldn't trust Grizzman. He needed help, but he couldn't take any chances with Dilly's life. "I must rescue Dilly right this second!" He ran to the mulberry bush, grabbed the 'Tude Boots, and jerked them on. His hands shook as he tied the laces.

"Wait here," Grizzman said. "I'll be right back."

Percy thought of scrambling away before anything disastrous could happen, but Grizzman seemed sincere.

Grizzman returned with a something wrapped in a piece of cloth. "Chocolate cream pie."

Percy tucked the pie in his tote. "Where'd you get it?"

"I grow cocoa plants. The butter's from my cows."

"Where'd you get the cows?"

"The Clumpie Farm."

"You stole a Clumpie cow? I thought you said you didn't steal animals."

"I don't. But I will rescue animals in need, give them a home. Also, I don't work my cows to death like the Clumpies. My cows relax. I give them time to ruminate. They're better off here with me. And I teach them tricks. Have you heard the rhyme about the cow who jumped over the moon?"

"Yes."

"That was one of my cows."

"Really, wow, that's a talented cow!" Percy saw the grizzled smile on Grizzman's face. "You're teasing me..."

"You're right, I'm joking. My cows are too content, and fat. They couldn't jump over a rock. I just wanted to lighten your mood. It's hard to think straight when you're agitated."

The more Percy talked to Grizzman, the less creepy he seemed.

"There are two ways to Shiny Shrine from here," Grizzman said, "the Skyward Path on the other side of the peak, then down the Stoney Steps—or for a faster way, you can cut diagonally through the forest."

"Which path is that?"

"There isn't one. You'll have to make your own."

"Then that's what I'll do. Thanks, Grizzman." Should he shake Grizzman's hand? Percy put his hands in his pockets instead.

"Good luck, Percy."

Percy bounced away in the 'Tude Boots. After a short distance, dark clouds dumped rain on his head. He didn't feel the cold, stinging drops. Lightning zinged overhead. He didn't notice. All his thoughts were on Dilly.

The rain dampened Percy's spirit—and his spring. The 'Tude Boots stuck in the mud, which made hopping too difficult. Percy slung the boots around his neck. He'd have to plod the old-fashioned way.

Plodding along, he slipped on the forest floor. Wet branches bopped him in the head. Rain seeped down his back. To keep himself company, he sang one of his mom's songs, Peg's favorite:

> Here we go making the bed,
> Here we go scratching our head,
> Here we go waving to Ed, Ted, and Fred,
> Tra la la la la

He envisioned the silly pantomimes his mom performed when she sang the song, and laughed. The sound of his own voice comforted him.

The rain pittered to a drizzle. The temperature dropped as the sky turned blacker. Percy's clothes froze to his body. He could hear the sound of frost crunching beneath his shoes as he plodded. He heard the sound of frost crunching when he was standing still. Maybe a tree branch had fallen? Maybe an animal was following him? Or was it something worse?

Percy plodded until he found a clearing. He plunked down on a tree stump to rest—cold, tired, and miserable. He felt a warm breeze, thought it smelled like chocolate. Then he remembered the treat in his totebag. He carefully unwrapped the pie, savoring each bite. It had been thoughtful of Grizzman to give him the pie. Maybe he would visit him when this ordeal was over. Grizzman wasn't a bad guy. But he was hard to look at. Percy shook his head. His attitude reminded him of Vic Brickhauser and the Malatete Twins rolled into one.

Percy had eaten half the pie when he realized that it was no time for eating! He bolted to his feet and headed across the clearing. He tripped over a root and fell forward. The next thing he knew, he was rolling down the mountain like one of Jericoe Jumpin Jupiter's big rubber balls. "Woooah!" Percy held onto his knees and tucked his chin to his chest. Clutching the totebag, he somersaulted through the forest.

Down and down he rolled . . .

Seventeen

Challenging Luster

THE WIND BLEW PERCY ON A zigzag course around trees and other obstacles. When the wind ceased, he rolled to a stop. He stood up covered in mud and moss. Rolling stones may gather no moss, but rolling boys do. Percy shook out his arms and legs. Before him were the Shiny Stairs. *How about that luck? A perfect roll. Onward to Dilly!*

The steps were partially visible in the darkness, the blackest night Percy had seen on the mountain. A dripping fog obscured the top of Shiny Stairs and oozed down like a misty blob. He started up, planting each foot cautiously on the slick steps. The fog descended on him like a veil. He couldn't see a thing. How was he supposed to find Dilly in this foggy mess? Maybe it was a trap. Maybe he should wait out the dark. Exhausted, Percy sat down on the steps to think. He closed his eyes. *Please be okay, Dilly, pleeease...*

❀ ❀ ❀

By the time Percy awoke the next morning, the fog was gone. A shard of light trickled down the stairs, injecting Percy with confidence. He devoured the rest of the chocolate pie, tucked in his shirt, and brushed the dried mud from his clothes. Ready for day number nine and ready to rescue Dilly!

Percy stomped up the second half of the stairs, through the courtyard, past the Luster statues. He called out for Dilly, whistled, and clapped his hands. No answer. He checked the fountain of fire, found his backpack, but not Dilly. Inside the shrine, he yelled and clapped again. He checked behind the throne, nothing. Percy ran back outside. "Dilly, Luster, where are you?"

There was only one place left to look—the Stoney Steps. At the thornbush gateway, the red eyes of the Biter Spiders glowed like hot coals. They looked more terrifying, their suckers bigger. He couldn't reach through the bush...couldn't do it...couldn't do it...

But he had to...had to...

"Nice spiders," Percy said. He reached to open the gate and felt something furry on his hand. A spider had wound a tentacle around his wrist. Percy screamed and whacked the spider against the gate. It fell off his arm. The other spiders raised their tentacles. Percy didn't wait to see what they would do. He shoved open the gate and charged up the Stoney Steps. Out of breath, he reached the last step.

He couldn't believe what he saw—a platoon of uniformed geese pulling the rope out of the tunnel! That wasn't supposed to happen. The rope was supposed to go in. *Grizzman had told the truth!*

The geese were commanded by an impressive goose, mighty in stature, with black feathers shiny as onyx. Its battle jacket was crowded with medallions, insignia, and epaulets. It wore a Cossack hat labeled "Captain Giles."

Captain Giles was perched atop the boulder partially covering the tunnel. He waved a saber around. "HONK YANK!" he honked.

"Honk stonk!" The platoon followed orders, tugged on the rope, pulling it out bit by bit. As the rope inched farther out of the tunnel, the sun dimmed another notch.

"Stop it!" Percy bolted to the tunnel. "You're ruining the light!" He grabbed onto the rope and tried to pull it away from the geese.

"HONK THONK THONK THONK!" Captain Giles said. The last row of geese flew in the air and dive-bombed at Percy. "Wonk thonk" filled the air. Using their powerful wings, the geese battered Percy away from the boulder. *Where is Valter when you need him?!*

Percy retreated to the stairs where he could hide and spy on the geese.

Now what? He needed Plan B. He grabbed the almonds from the totebag, and as much as he hated to part with food, lobbed them at the geese. They bounced off their beaks. Tossing vegetables on his vegetable farm had paid off. Lunging for the nuts, the geese dropped the rope. Next, he tossed handfuls of kumquats at them. Bonk, bonk, bonk.

"HONK HALT!"

The geese continued feeding. Next, Percy pinged their heads with chocolate cherries. The geese enjoyed them honkingly.

Captain Giles opened his beak wide to honk an order. Percy dug in his pocket, found the pea Peg had given him. It was hard as a marble. He hurled it down the commander's throat, choking him.

Captain Giles gagged until he dislodged the pea. "HONK STONK!" The geese platoon finally ruffled to attention.

"FLAP AND FLY!"

The geese platoon saluted and flew away, followed by Captain Giles. Percy raced down the steps to Luster's courtyard just as the geese waddled into Shiny Shrine. Sneaking inside, he saw Luster slouched on his throne.

Captain Giles stood rigid. "Daily report, sir!"

"Giles, have you completed your orders?" asked Luster.

"No, sir! Production has stopped."

"Beejeebies!" Luster said. "And how much longer until the rope is completely pulled from the tunnel?"

"An hour or two, sir!"

Luster grimaced. "That confounded sun is holding out longer than I'd thought. Problems, problems! I should be controlling the light by now!" Luster pulled on his jaw. "I've got enough problems. Like Percy from Yoosa. I have to make sure he is annihilated. Can you believe that twit kid?" In a falsetto voice, Luster said, "I need to pull the sun back in, to save the light for Yoosa. And everything can be peaceful again!"

Giles ha-ha-honked.

"Over my lardy-dardy body!" Luster said. "Are you getting this, Giles, you drudge? You must hurry! Work your platoon harder! No rest! Fulfill your duty, or I'll cook your goose! Understood?"

"Understood. However, there might be one impediment."

"Pray tell, what?"

"Grizzman. He could appear and blow away the platoon, sir."

"I fixed that problem, Giles. The twit kid should have engaged in bloody combat with Grizzman by now. Maybe I'll get lucky and they're both dead."

Percy stepped forward. "Not exactly," he said.

"Beejeebies! You're alive!" Luster's face contorted. He gritted his teeth; the rubies blazed. "Giles, meet Percy." Giles dipped his beak. "My heavens, twit kid, but you're filthy," Luster said. "Ever heard of bathing? By the way, how dead is Grizzman?"

"Not dead at all."

"Not even a little bit?"

"No."

"Why the beejeebies not?!"

"He didn't steal my dog."

"What difference does that make? He's a hideously deformed mammal who shouldn't be allowed to live. Who wants to look at that thing?"

"That's a bad attitude."

"Tut tut, twit. I call it practical. Like my next trick."

Geese soldiers wheeled in a cart with a wooden cage on top. Inside, Percy could see a fuzzy blur. It was Dilly, running around in circles with a terrified look on his face.

"Dilly!" screamed Percy, but Dilly kept circling.

"He's a nutty pup," Luster said.

"Dilly, it's me!" Percy whistled, clapped his hands.

Dilly stopped. He stuck his snout through the bars, panted hard. His tongue hung out; his eyes looked bleary.

"I'm here to get you, Dilly." Percy glared at Luster. "Let Dilly go right now!"

"Are you as nutty as your dog? I've been working on my plan for a long time. I hate sunlight and I have to make it vanish. Then, with my control of fire, I'll control the people. And all their farms—all of Yoosa."

"Why would you want to do that?"

"That's what I do, oppress and rule."

"What makes you think you're allowed to do that?"

"I'm entitled. I've given myself a title: 'Fire Emperor.' Bow down to your ruler."

"No," Percy said. "What did the sun say to the ruler?"

"I don't know. What?"

"You play with fire, you get burned."

"That's not funny," Luster said.

"It's not supposed to be."

"Well, if you're trying to scare me, pardon me if I don't shake. I might lose my rubies. Giles, fetch another cage."

"Wait!"

"What now?"

"It's not polite to put people and dogs in cages."

Luster gave Percy a ho-hum look. "The wealthy and powerful don't have to be polite."

"You also fool people."

"Of course, why not? I come from a long line of Foolems."

"And you lied about promising to help me."

"Don't you know that people are born liars?! You *are* as nutty as your dog. And a plebian pecksniffish ninnyhammer to boot! Give me lardy-dardyness any day!"

Plebian—what? Where was Philious Mot when you needed him?

Luster stomped his foot. The platoon honked and stonked, seizing Percy and stuffing him into a cage. Percy thought: *These geese are vorth getting vrid of.*

Luster danced around the cages with a torch. He chanted, "Beejeebies, beejeebies, you little creepies! Ashes to asher, dust to duster, all will belong to Luster!"

Bad rhyming. (Badly in need of Bard's help.) Even worse dancing. Luster looked like a sweaty jellyfish twirling a baton—so dumb that Percy forgot for a moment to be afraid. Even Dilly looked amused.

Luster continued to sweat. Perspiration dripped down his head, washing away a mask from his face. Then his purple robe slipped off, revealing...

"EGADS!"

Beneath the mask was a wrinkly slimy face with a flat nose and round mouth. Underneath the robe was an emaciated gelatinous body with shriveled appendages.

Dilly barked ferociously. Percy stared, thinking Luster needed to visit Udell Woodruff for arm and leg work.

"It's rude to stare!" Luster said.

"Are...you...human?" Percy asked.

"Half."

"What's the other half?"

"Worm."

Dilly went berserk, barking nonstop, charging at the bars with all his might.

"I've never heard of that combination," Percy said.

"You'd be surprised how many humans are really half worm," Luster said. "Any law farmers in Yoosa?"

"No," said Percy.

"Too bad," said Luster.

"My dad says we don't need them because Yoosians are civil people."

"Nonsense. If you ever meet one, check him out. You'll see what I'm talking about."

Percy kept gawking. "I'm sorry for your—"

"Sorry for what? Invertebrates are a proud species–leeches, parasitic tapeworms, the whole glob of us. I enjoy worminess, worming around the rules, worming to my advantage." Luster sneered. "We're made to slither. And we're efficient at it. We're the most numerous animal on earth. And for good reason. It's no fluke that worms haven't evolved for millions of years." Luster laughed his rascally laugh. "I like not having my own backbone. I don't have to stand up for anything. My mother never had to say to me, 'Stand up straight.' The only backbone

I have is the one I inserted into my robe. Worminess is underrated!" he bellowed. "Although I do give humans credit for their big teeth and hands. Beneficial to chew things up and spit 'em out. And to grab what you want. That's why I'm half and half."

"Where did you get the backbone?" asked Percy.

"From a bell farmer."

"What happened to him?"

"What do you think? I rang his bell! But let's get back to the main topic here. I have to get rid of you two dodos so I can triumph in my quest to control all of Yoosa."

"What about Grizzman?"

"He's ancient. He'll die soon enough. But it's your turn now. Shall we begin?" With the torch, Luster lit the wooden bars of the cages. Flames shot up to the gilded ceiling and reflected off the mirrors. The shrine looked as if it were ablaze. The pungent odor of smoke filled the room. Percy and Dilly crouched in the center of their cages. They coughed, then gagged, then began to suffocate, gasping for air. Luster chortled in his wormy glory.

A puff of wind blew into the shrine. Then a gust. Then a blast!

Then Grizzman! Peering through the smoke, Percy saw the outline of his galootish body lumbering to the stage.

Grizzman blew a gale of wind around the shrine, snuffing out the torches and sending Luster airborne. Luster flew from the stage and ricocheted along the sword fence. Grizzman took another big breath and blew on both cages, extinguishing the fires. Clouds of thick black smoke filled the air. Grizzman pulled the bars off the cages and helped Percy and Dilly to freedom.

Dilly jumped into Percy's arms. Percy held him tight. "I missed you..."

"Ruff..."

"I missed you..."

"Ruff..."

Luster cowered on the ground. "Fight on, geese platoon! Fight to the death!"

With Captain Giles in the lead, the geese dive-bombed Grizzman, but he blew them away with one powerful breath. He blew again so hard that their feathers ripped off and their wings bent backward.

"HONK STOOOONNKKKK!"

Grizzman blew the geese into a fluffy whirlwind—out of the shrine, across the courtyard, and down the Shiny Steps, where they landed in a feathery heap.

In the courtyard, Grizzman scooped up a handful of sand and threw it onto the Fountain of Fire. He blew hard until a glob of liquid glass formed. Percy watched in awe. Luster hid behind the Fountain of Fire, Dilly standing guard and growling at him. Grizzman added more sand and blew a steady stream of air, forming an immense glass bubble. He snagged Luster by the back of his neck.

"Beejeebies...nnooooo..."

Grizzman dropped Luster inside the huge bubble, then blew until the top sealed shut. The glass hardened and Luster was suspended inside, unable to squirm more than a few inches.

"That takes care of him," Grizzman said, as casually as if he'd been strolling in the park.

"You saved our lives!"

"Ruff!"

"What a handsome dog you have, Percy." Grizzman stooped to pet Dilly.

"Grizzman, the geese might come back. Why didn't you get rid of them for good?"

"They've been under a bad influence, that's all. I just wanted to get them out of the way. Besides, there are probably goslings around some-where." Grizzman carried the glass bubble into the shrine and set it on the throne. "Now Luster can stare at himself in the mirrors for the rest of his life. He won't be going anywhere ever again."

Percy smiled. Dilly's ears wagged from side to side.

Luster banged on the glass, smearing it with his slimy arms. His pleas for help could barely be heard.

"We have something more important to do," Grizzman said. "Follow me."

Eighteen

Seizing the Sun

ON THE MOUNTAIN SUMMIT, Grizzman grappled with the metallic rope. Little by little he pulled the sun closer, slowly undoing the damage done by the geese platoon. The sky brightened, as if an army of candles were marching across it. The sun seemed glad to be closer to Yoosa. Even though tethered by the rope, it spun and leapt, performing a dazzling ballet.

Dilly untangled the rope while Percy pushed it into the tunnel. The three labored without stopping, energized by the sun. Percy put on his sunglasses and another pair on Dilly. He'd almost forgotten what a sunny day looked like, or what a hot summer day felt like. Excitement zinged through his body. "Hurry, Grizzman, hurry!" he said. "Keep pulling!"

"Slow and steady, Percy," Grizzman said. "The rope is old and frayed. I don't want to take any chances. It might snap in two. Then we'd lose the sun forever."

"Slow and steady, Grizzman," Percy said. "Like plodding—and plodding works."

"Percy, could you do me a favor and call me Barry?"

"Okay, Grizz...I mean, Barry." *Don't forget, it's Barry from now on,* Percy said to himself. Barry was a better name for him—much nicer.

❋ ❋ ❋

All day Barry pulled the rope. Instead of the sunlight fading in the afternoon, the sky remained bright. Barry tugged on the rope and let go. "That's it for now," he said. "Let the sun revolve on its own." He explained to Percy that he needed to calibrate the exact distance the sun should be from Yoosa at a certain time of day for that time of year; otherwise, he could end up altering the seasons and weather forever. "In the morning, I'll make final adjustments to make sure the sun is aligned correctly."

"We're almost finished?" Percy said. "One more night on the mountain and we can go home? I can't wait!"

"Ruff!"

"You and Dilly can camp here," Barry said, "or you're welcome to stay in my cabin. I'll fix us a meal."

Percy was so worn out from the Luster incident, he welcomed the rest and the food. He knew Dilly would, too.

Dinner consisted of white waffles, walnut bread and cheese, huckleberries, and fresh milk. For dessert, Barry proudly served chocolate cake on a pretty ceramic plate.

"How do you know so much about the sun and weather?" Percy asked.

"I read books."

"I like to read, too," Percy said. "Where do you get your books?"

"From the book farmer."

"Me, too!"

"Only Mr. Page probably knows who you are."

"What do you mean?"

"The first book I ever got, and that was a *long* time ago, I snitched from Mr. Page's great-grandfather's wagon. In its place, I left a box of chocolates. After that, Old Man Page would leave a book in his wagon and I'd swap it for chocolate. I did the same thing with Old Man Page's son, then the grandson, and now the great-grandson."

Percy thought a moment. "Wow, Barry, you must be really old!"

"That I am, Percy, that I am. It's genetics, unusual ones, you might say." He added softly, "Like why I have so many lumps."

Nothing wrong with that Percy thought. He remembered Grandpap had said Dilly had unusual genetics. "What are those glass orbs on the table?"

"I'm trying to invent a new light source," Barry said. "First, I tried to find a way to trap sunlight in a bottle, so that way, if the sun went away, or if a bad person made it disappear, we would still have light. But the sun's rays only shine when they're released from the sun. They aren't storable. And that's when I got the idea of making artificial light."

"Like a candle."

"Yes, but stronger, and longer-lasting. I rigged a system using the windmill which rotates a wheel made of metal wires and magnets..."

Percy yawned. His eyelids felt heavy. Dilly had already curled up in the corner of the room. The drone of his snoring lulled Percy into a sleepy trance. He missed Barry's explanation about how a current lights up a filament in the glass orb and how...

One more day, one more day...

At dawn on the tenth day of his journey, Percy watched the sun rise from the mountaintop. He, Barry, and Dilly stood silent while a gorgeous day emerged. Based on his scientific calculations, Barry made the last adjustment to the rope's length. Then he looped it around and around the boulder to hold it in place.

"Percy, can you help me secure the rope? It mustn't come loose."

"I have an idea," Percy said. He retrieved the giant ball of dental floss from his backpack. He ran around the boulder dozens of times, wrapping the floss over the rope until the boulder looked like a waxy iceberg. "I doubt anyone can untie the rope now."

"I think you're right," Barry said. "Ready for the last part?"

With all their might, Barry, Percy, and Dilly rolled the boulder over the opening of the tunnel and sealed it shut.

"There she glows," Barry said.

"The sun is fixed?"

"Yes."

"We really did it?"

"Yes."

"Bobbydazzler!"

"It sure is a dazzler."

"Rrruuufff!" Dilly's ears flopped up and down.

Percy waited for the sky to part and trumpets to sound. For a choir of crickets to sing. For an equestrian cavalcade. For a marching band. But no such fanfare. "That's great, Barry. Just great. My mom and dad, Auntie, Grandpap, everybody in Yoosa will be happy." Shouldn't he be happier? He just wanted to go home.

"Percy, what you did—coming here to fix the sun—was very brave. When you face adversity, it's hard to be brave at your age—or any age."

"It's a good thing I didn't know what to expect. And a good thing my aunt told me about the plod, and that you were here to help me. You're a good friend, Barry."

Barry looked pleased, then somber. "You'll be leaving now?"

"Soon as we can."

"Ruff!"

"Why don't you come with us?" Percy said. "You can stay at my house."

Barry shook his head. The spiky hair on his face blurred together.

"And all the vegetables you could want, Barry."

"No, thanks."

"I know what you mean."

"It's not the vegetables, Percy. I don't belong in Yoosa. Some people don't fit in."

"I know what you mean."

"Amethyst Mountain is my home. But I'm glad we could meet. I don't meet many people."

"It would help if you didn't wear a bear costume to scare them away."

Barry smiled. "Let me show you a different transportation method down the mountain, one that I use when I go to Yoosa to collect things. I call it the Cylinder-Mobile. You can use it anytime you want. It will save you traveling time."

Barry's invention was a glass tube large enough to seat six regular-sized people (or two if you were the size of Barry carrying a cow). It sloped in front for optimal aerodynamics, had a latched door on top with a sliding window, and two benches inside. The bottom of the Cylinder-Mobile fit onto an iron rail which traversed the entire length of the mountain. It operated by the force of gravity. A device in front controlled speed—a rubber pad attached by two springs. Using your feet to push the pad against the rail caused the vehicle to decelerate.

"How do you get the vehicle back up the mountain?" asked Percy.

Barry pointed to a cable above them, running parallel to the rail. "I stand up in the Cylinder-Mobile through the window. Then I grab the cable, and hand-over-hand, I pull myself back up."

"I'm glad we're going down and not up," Percy said. In the Cylinder-Mobile, he practiced operating the rubber pad. "Ready to go!"

Barry closed the overhead door.

"Bye, Barry, thanks for everything!" Percy said. Dilly waved his ears.

Barry gave the Cylinder-Mobile a shove. "Come back soon," yelled Barry. But Percy was too far down the line to hear. Barry blew into the sky. Clouds formed into a sentence: "Plod On."

The Cylinder-Mobile glided down the mountain like a wagon hitched to a draft horse. Percy controlled the speed for a smooth ride. Through the glass, Percy and Dilly watched the mountainside rush by.

Halfway down Amethyst Mountain, they heard Yoosians hooting and hollering. The closer they got to the bottom, the louder the cheers grew.

"Hooray! There's the sun!"

"Yahoo! The sun is back!"

"Yippee! Celebrate the sun!"

The Cylinder-Mobile coasted to a stop at the end of the line, the edge of Yoosa's foothills. Percy unlatched the door and climbed out. Dilly catapulted out. Percy slowly breathed in, held his breath, and exhaled. It was good to be back! They walked toward the town center. Dot Dash telegraphed the arrival.

As Yoosians saw them approaching, they ran to greet them, cheering even louder. "Percy, you saved the day!" they called out. More people gathered. They formed a circle around Percy, so many people he couldn't see them all. He smiled with what little energy he had left. Dilly wagged his ears.

"Good job, young'un!" Bronco Snozhead said, slapping Percy on the back.

Mrs. Tubula handed him a bagel. "Was there enough food to eat on that mountain, honey?" she asked.

"Were there any monsters?"

"Any chickens?"

Percy was too exhausted to talk. He wanted to lie down and sleep for a month.

"Speech, Percy, speech!"

"Tell us everything that happened!"

"Can't it wait?" asked Percy.

"Noooooo!"

Percy saw the excitement on everyone's faces. "All right, here's what happened: first, a walk not for a miser, but of misery. We had to plod, plod, plod. Then we landed in Stinko Swamp. *Groistayoba!* Valter Vulture helped us out. Then plod, plod, plod on the Trail of Trees with 'Boo hoo hoo' and 'Think pink' by the Bird Brigade. Then into Honey Tears Gulch and more plod, plod, plodding."

Mrs. Yin whispered, "Do you think he ate funny mushrooms up there?"

"Then whimsey woo, Droll Troll. Dilly answered the question and we crossed his bridge. And then Natsy Gnat wanted to eat us for dinner. Harrruumph!" Percy sped up the pace. "Then we plodded through the Course of Colors. Then we met Fuddy and Duddy, who confused us. Ickugg! Then on to Shiny Shrine where Luster Krupter lived. Beejeebies! Then came the worst part..."

"Grizzz...mann?" stammered Old Man Pops.

"No, Dilly gets stolen."

Jaws dropped. "Oh, no!"

Percy continued at a faster clip. "Then Ima gave me 'Tude Boots and optimism to go to Barry Grizzman's cabin to get Dilly. Except Dilly wasn't there. And, by the way, Barry Grizzman is very nice, and a hero, too. Then, back to Luster where Dilly was held prisoner in a cage. The geese platoon attacked me, and Luster tried to burn us alive, and..."

"My stars!"

"My word!""

"Weren't you scared out of your wits?"

"I lost my wits a long time before that," Percy said. He talked as fast as he could. "Barry blew a windstorm and rescued Dilly and me. He blew away the geese platoon. He blew a big glass bubble and put Luster inside it so he can never get out." In one breath, Percy said, "Barry pulled the rope to the sun and we anchored it in place and now the sun has returned to Yoosa and Dilly and I cruised down the mountain in the Cylinder-Mobile and here we are." Percy exhaled. "Can I go home now?"

"That's the best story I ever heard! You ought to write a book," Mr. Page said.

"You're a titan," Kay Oss said.

"I'm astonished at the epic nature of your odyssey," Bard Leary said.

"You're valiant, valorous, unvanquishable," Philious Mot said.

"I think we should have a Percy Statue in the park," said one of the Pettifog Fogies.

"I'm composing a symphony called *Amethyst Summer,*" Maestro Muzacky said.

"Plodding works. Who would have thought?"

"Can a *cat* do it?" asked Miss Fellini.

"Can you teach me to plod?" asked Biff Stuffy.

"No, teach me first!" Vic Brickhauser said.

"Anyone can plod," said Percy. "You don't need lessons."

"Yes, but what's the secret?"

"There's no secret. Just one step forward, and then another. And keep going. You conquer by continuing."

The crowd oohed and aahed.

"Here, here, fellow Yoosians," Mayor Oscar said, working his way to the front of the crowd. "Since we're all gathered together on this auspicious occasion, I'd like to take this opportunity to tell you about my idea to implement a crisis management program to deal with…"

"Might I politely ask you to put a sock in it, Mayor?" Rocky Cardia said, politely.

"Or dental floss," Buckminster Dent said.

"Who needs your programs, Mayor, when we have Percy?"

"Three cheers for Percy!"

Applause broke out. Was it Percy's imagination, or did everyone seem nicer than before?

"Applaud the plod! Applaud the plod!" the crowd chanted.

Percy could still hear the crowd cheering as he shuffled home, too pooped to plod.

Nineteen

The Homecoming

OME AT LAST IN THEIR oh-so-comfortable beds! While Percy and Dilly slept, Mrs. Veerance prepared a welcome-home feast from special recipes concocted in her laboratory. At lunchtime, she set the plank table with her best dishes and bowls. Everything was ready—except the guests of honor, who were still snoozing.

Mr. Veerance took his place at the table. "Percy deserves the extra sleep," he said.

"Perrrr!" squealed Peg. Two tufts of hair jiggled.

Mrs. Veerance set out a pitcher of raspberry juice. "Percy likes this better than mushroom juice—I think," she said.

"Shroom, shroom," Peg said. She poked a finger in the alfalfa sprout soufflé, then licked it.

They waited.

Mr. Veerance and Peg played a game with mung beans. Mrs. Veerance folded and refolded her napkin. Mr. Veerance chewed on a carrot stick. Mrs. Veerance hummed a tune. Peg ate the mung beans. They waited. Lunchtime passed.

Finally, Percy meandered into the kitchen. His head felt hazy. The setting was familiar, but his memory of Amethyst Mountain was so strong, he expected to be plodding through a craggy crevasse any minute.

"Perrr!" Peg said.

"Huh?" Percy focused toward the plank table, recognizing his family. "Hi, Peg. Hi, Mom." He yawned. "Hi, Dad." His dad's hair didn't seem as orange.

"Are you hungry, Son?"

"It's time to eat! Have a seat. You're in for a treat," Mrs. Veerance said in a sing-songy voice.

He was starved. Anything besides a mold delicacy sounded good to Percy. He plunked down on a stool. Peg crawled across the table and hung onto Percy's neck. "Now I have a Peg neck," he said. He kissed her chubby cheek and wiped bean gunk off his lips. Something cooking in the oven smelled good. Percy saw his mom smile at him. She looked happy. So did his dad.

"It's good to be home, Mom and Dad," Percy said. He meant it.

"Ruff!" Dilly trotted through the kitchen and plopped under Percy's stool.

"While you were gone, Percy dear, Flora told me you like meat pies," Mrs. Veerance said. "I never knew that. Why didn't you tell me?"

"I did."

"Well, guess what we're having to eat?"

"Alfalfa sprouts soufflé?"

"No, that's for Peg. *You're* having meat pie."

"What kind of meat? It's not vulture, is it?"

"No, dear, it's turkey."

"Is that all right with you, Percy?" asked Mr. Veerance. "Because if not, I can run over to the Bovines and get a T-bone. All the farmers are trading with me now."

"Turkey pie is fine, Dad. And I'll have some carrots. And peas, too." Percy loaded his plate, plus one for Dilly. He took a big forkful of turkey pie. "Mmmm, the pie is tasty, Mom." *What a difference ten days makes.*

"Maybe I'll serve it again tomorrow night. We're having a small dinner party."

"Who's coming?" Percy asked.

"So far there's Flora, Linus, Grandpap, the Kismets, the Ewings and their little Mary, Zoe and Biff, Mrs. Pepperaji, and Bard. Maybe one or two more."

That didn't sound like a small dinner party to Percy. But he was glad Mary Ewing was coming. He was going to say "hi" to her. "In case I forget, Mom, remind me to tell Mr. Kismet where he can find a big pile of feathers for his quilts."

"Okay, dear. Everyone wants to hear all about your jaunt up the mountain."

"It was more than a jaunt, wasn't it, son?"

Percy nodded. It was a huge, plodding, exciting, difficult, stinky, scary, enlightening jaunt. (To be explained later when his brain wasn't so muddled.)

"For dessert, I've made banana ice cream. Peg, darling, quit smashing beans in your hair. You should see all the trading your father has done at the Xotic Farm."

Percy squelched his shock. "That's great, Dad." *What a difference ten days make!*

Mr. Veerance said quietly, "I wish I would have had it in me to go up the mountain."

"What are those purple stalks you left on the counter?" asked Mrs. Veerance.

"It's wild celery for Peg."

Peg squealed.

"You've had plenty to eat, Peg," Mr. Veerance said. "But a little more won't hurt!" He gave her the bunch.

Peg crunched away.

"Percy, do you think I could make toothpaste out of the celery?"

"Sure, Dad. It tastes like grapes."

"What are those muddy plant things you left outside, dear? Should I throw them away?"

"No, Mom, those are 'Tude Boots. I want to show them to Mr. Abu. And I brought back some huckleberries for Mona."

"You'll have to wait to give them to her. She's on a date," Mrs. Veerance said.

"A date?" Percy's eyes widened. "Like a boy-girl thing?"

"Yes, that kind."

"A date with who?"

"Clyde Dale, Mr. Fowler's horse. It's their second one. Your aunt is chaperoning. Flora fixed Mona's mane all pretty with daisies in it."

"You should see Mona now," Mr. Veerance said, "a clippety-clack in her trot."

Percy grinned. *What a difference ten days make.*

"Keep eating, Percy, dear. You're a growing boy," Mrs. Veerance said. "And I have something else for you—a song I wrote for your home-coming, called *Cantata for Percival*. While you were gone, I traded fried potato strips with tomato gravy for singing lessons with Maestro

Muzacky." Mrs. Veerance tapped her glass with a fork and sang "Mee mee mee" to warm up her throat. Her eyebrows started to wrinkle. She smoothed them out with her fingertips. She clasped her hands at her bosom and opened her mouth. Out came a pleasant soprano voice—on key. She sang about a perky turkey who couldn't fly and ended up in a meat pie. Near the end of the song, she raised her arms in the air and belted out the last note for thirty seconds (but it seemed much longer). The glasses rattled. Mrs. Veerance looked gleeful. The rest of the family looked stunned.

Mr. Veerance finally broke the silence. "Egads, Vera, fantastic! You're better than Gence crickets!"

"Nice song, Mom," Percy said. "Now you can be Vera Veerance, V.C.S.—for 'Very Capable Singer.'"

Mrs. Veerance beamed.

Out of the corner of his eye, Percy saw his dad sneaking peeks at him. He finished eating, nothing hidden in his napkin.

"Percy..." Mr. Veerance hesitated. "That was something you did, hiking all the way up Amethyst Mountain and fixing the sun. Really something."

"Thanks, Dad. But I had help." Soon Percy planned to tell his parents about Barry Grizzman, and how Barry had rescued him and Dilly—and the sun. And how he'd like his friend to come for a visit and stay with them.

"While you were away," Mr. Veerance said, "I got you some books from the book farmer."

"And a coloring book for Peg," Mrs. Veerance said.

"We don't have any colored pencils."

"We do now."

Mr. Veerance handed the book to Percy. "It's about a young man who goes off on a quest, like you did."

Percy read the title: *The Legend of Indivi.* He liked the cover with a picture of a warrior and a castle on it. "Looks like a good story."

"You can read it as slowly as you want."

Percy slipped the book in his back pocket. "I need to go to Grandpap's farm."

"Now?"

"Yes."

"For crickets?"

"Something else."

"But you'll see him tomorrow night."

"I need to check on something today."

"Aren't you tired?"

"I've been sleeping all day."

"It's getting late," Mrs. Veerance said.

"There's still sunlight," Percy said.

"Thanks to you. Sure, Son. You can go."

"When I get back, Dad, want to swat some flies?"

At the Gence Cricket Farm, an assortment of dogs rounded up swarms of crickets as if they were herding sheep, shooing them inside the cricket compound. With three sets of legs, crickets could run fast. Grandpap told Percy that the crickets had just returned from an outing in the country, where they had basked in the sunlight and warmed their wings. "They have a surprise for you, Percy," he said, "as a way to thank you for bringing the sun back."

Percy and Dilly sat on a compound wall to watch the performance. A quartet of females played a violin concerto. Then a group of males sang an operetta. Grandpap Gence beamed with pride. "Yoosa is alive with the sound of music tonight," he said.

At the dogs' house, a mixture of mutts barked greetings to Percy and Dilly. Lady Jane, a short but stately dachshund/mutt/gherkin, scooted over to them.

"Where are your pups, Lady Janie?" Percy said, scratching her ears. "Are there any that look like a velvet cucumber?"

In the back of the pen, four pups huddled together like pickles in a jar. Percy picked up the smallest one, brown and fuzzy with floppy ears, a long snout, and a lump for a tail. "What do you think, Dill?"

"Ruff!"

"You're right, she's perfect."

The next morning, Percy pulled on his overalls, laced up his work boots, and was ready for picking vegetables. He'd missed doing chores. They might be hard, dirty, even boring, but the chores were his job—and doing them benefited his family.

Mr. Veerance told Percy the vegetables could wait and to take a few days off because the weather was magnificent. He suggested Percy and Dilly swim at Lake Cheery, picnic at Yoosa Park, or play with the other farm kids.

"Maybe I will, Dad," Percy said. "I started reading the book you gave me. It's really good."

"If you want another one, let me know. We can take a trip to Mr. Page's farm. And by the way, Son, you pick vegetables real good."

But first things first. Percy and Dilly raced through the fields at the edge of the Veerance farm. Percy cradled the puppy in a sling across his chest. In the distance, he could see Auntie Flora kneeling in a furrow of flowers. A sunflower visor was tilted over her forehead. She stacked bunches of white, pink, and blue asters.

"Steady plodding brings prosperity!" Percy yelled.

Flora looked up. "Is that Percy Veerance, Prince of Plod?!" She tossed a bouquet of asters into the air. Petals fluttered down like confetti. "I missed you like the dickens!"

"Ruff!"

"You, too, Dilly. Steady plodding bring prosperity?"

"Just like you said."

"Everyone is absolutely thrilled with having the sun back," Flora said. "So thrilled they're trading for flowers like crazy. What a difference a sunlit day makes! When I made my deliveries today, I didn't hear one single complaint. And over at the Happy Clown Farm, the clowns are laughing! You did a wonderful thing, Percy."

"I couldn't have done it without your advice, Auntie."

"How's it feel to be home?"

"Great—but different. You'll see for yourself at the dinner party tonight. Not only will the food be good, but so will the singing!"

"Unbelievable," Flora said.

"Know what else is unbelievable? My dad's trading at the Xotic fruit farm."

"There are big changes all over Yoosa. Right now I want to hear everything that happened on your journey. Don't leave anything out. Why did it take so long? How did you rope the sun in? Did you see Ima? Anything scary? Any flowers? Did you have enough—" Flora stopped talking, pointed to the sack on Percy's chest. "What's that?"

Percy folded back the sling, exposing the pup's head. Her eyes were closed, her snout resting on her pudgy tummy. "She's part of what I have to tell you about."

Flora put her arm around Percy. "Let's go inside. We'll have food and drink and a good story."

They spent all day at Flora's cottage. Dilly chewed the furniture. Flora was enthralled by Percy's tale. At the end, she said, "There's something to be said about choosing the right path."

Percy didn't need to look at her to know her eyebrows were in the up position. "Another thing I want to talk to you about, Auntie. How about we go next week?"

"Go where?"

"Up the mountain."

"You're joking, right?"

Twenty

⊱Plod On

O N A CLOUDLESS SUNLIT DAY the following week, they began their trip, plodding across the Yoosa farmlands, through the backwoods, and up the foothills to the base of Amethyst Mountain. Percy carried the pup in his backpack; Dilly trotted ahead. Flora wore a pansy bonnet, her thinking cap, so she could concentrate on the adventure at hand.

Along the way, Flora told Percy that while he was gone she had happened upon a stupendous bird snared in one of Mr. Fowler's traps. She immediately set him free. "He was not your average wild bird," Flora said. "He was a gentleman and well spoken. He offered to fly me anywhere I wished to travel. And that's how we're going up the mountain today."

Percy heard a flapping sound in the distance.

"Here comes my new friend now," Flora said.

The flapping grew louder. It sounded like flying elephants. The air swirled in torrents.

"Groistayoba!"

"I'd know that voice anywhere!" Percy said.

In a rush of wind, Valter landed beside Flora. He removed his top hat and bowed. "At your service, Miss Flora."

"Valter!"

"Ruff!"

"Hello, Percy. Hello, Dilly. Vonderful to see you again."

"You know my aunt?"

"Ve made fast acquaintance. Pole-ite woman. And charming. A friend vhen I vas in need. I could have ended up in vulture potpie. How vrude! But Miss Flora liberated me from that horrible fate. And now I am honored to provide her transportation." Valter fluttered his wings and lifted from the ground. "Vready for your flight?" In one talon, Valter gripped Percy's shirt collar. In the other, he clutched Dilly's neck. In his beak, he held onto Flora's belt. Valter beat his wings and up they went, soaring through the sunny sky.

As they flew over Amethyst Mountain, Percy pointed to the paths he and Dilly had plodded on and the places where they'd camped. He spied a kaleidoscope of colors. "Down there, Valter, land there!"

They touched down at the entrance to the Course of Colors. "This place is vorth seeing," Valter said.

"Thanks for the ride, Valter," Percy said.

"Lovely way to travel," Flora said.

"Call on me anytime," Valter said.

"You should start your own flying business."

"Yes, flying my in-laws out of town. But I must leave now. I have crack in glass to fix. Another time I will fly you vay to top—to see fascinating spectacle. Until next time."

"Hold on to your hat, Auntie!" Percy escorted Flora on a grand tour of the Course of Colors. He anticipated she would be at her dreamiest, and he was right. They slowly proceeded through each section. Flora absorbed the colorful marvel, exclaiming "Wonderful!" over and over.

In the purple glen, they rested on a wisteria bench and ate boysenberry muffins. Flora said she was astounded. She recited all the names of the flowers and shrubs like a prayer. "This place is nature's sanctuary," she said. "The colors, the fragrances—the whole atmosphere makes me feel enraptured! And that gives me a wonderful idea. I'm going to duplicate this maze at home. Then Yoosians can walk through it and experience its therapeutic effect. Their spirits will be lifted! I'll call it Super-Natural Land."

Next on the travel itinerary: Zeal Crater. The group boarded the Cylinder-Mobile, which somehow had been parked conveniently outside the gazebo at the end of the Course of Colors. Percy told his aunt that Barry had said he could use the vehicle anytime he was on the mountain. They leisurely cruised downward, Flora with her face plastered to the window. "I want to ride all over the mountain in this contraption," she said. "What incredible scenery!"

They rolled to a stop at the edge of the crater and climbed out of the vehicle. They walked the short distance to Ima's house. Percy noticed a lump in the middle of the crater and made a mental note to himself to ask Ima about it.

Sitting on the front porch in a rocking chair—reading a book entitled *Astrophysics for Astrophysicists and Dodos*—was a dignified-looking bird in a tweed jacket. Corduroy pants were hiked up over his plump tummy. He wore sandals showing off his splay-toed feet.

"You must be Numen," Percy said.

"Indubitably." He sprang from the rocker on tiny legs. "Percy, I presume?" Numen spoke with an eloegant voice. "And Miss Flora, too? Jovial day. Ima will be most elated to see you." Waddling, he ushered them inside the house.

Ima's eyes and freckles twinkled. She giggled. "I sense something lovely—could it be my dear friend?"

"I love the Course of Colors, I love the Course of Colors," Flora said over and over, hugging Ima.

"It's splendid to see you," Flora said.

"Wish I could say the same," Ima said. They both laughed.

"We must visit more often!"

Numen made tea, which he served with chocolate-covered strawberries. "May I offer my gratitude to you, Percy, for fixing the sun?"

"I had help," Percy said.

"You mean the plod?"

"Yes, and a friend, too."

"Then my thanks to both of you. Warmth and light are not only a pleasure to have around, but a necessity as well."

Flora and Ima had not seen each other for years and it seemed to Percy, they made up for it by talking for what seemed like years. They discussed building a flower maze in Yoosa, shared edible flower recipes, and exchanged gardening tips.

Hurry up and catch up! Percy was anxious to get to their last destination. While Dilly and the pup napped on the divan, Numen showed Percy the book room. Like Ima, Numen had read all the books.

"Which one is your favorite?" Percy asked.

"*The Chortling Brook.* It's a story of a pixie who discovers the power of a stream to make people laugh, and it changes their lives forever. It was one of Ima's favorite books as a child."

"Ima likes to laugh, doesn't she?" Percy said.

"Indubitably. She says that's when she knows she's alive. She even laughs about being blind."

"How did she get blind?"

"Ima's father was an archer. One day while he was at target practice and Ima was painting landscapes on the target range...well, you know what happens when you poke a sharp stick in your eye."

Percy flinched.

"Would you like to read—" A pounding on the door interrupted Numen. "I'll answer it, Ima." Numen waddled from the book room.

"Flora," Ima said, "I'm expecting a friend. Will you join us for cream cakes?"

Percy looked at Flora and shook his head.

"I'm sorry to cut our visit short," Flora said, "but Percy has one more place to show me today."

The pounding continued. Dilly jetted to the door. He wagged his ears.

"Patience, please, I'm waddling as fast as I can," Numen said as he opened the door.

On the porch stood a big galoot with a big smile to match—Barry.

"Bobbydazzler!" Barry wasn't hairy anymore!

"Hi, Percy. Hi, Dilly." Barry scratched Dilly's head.

"Ruff!"

Percy pulled Barry inside. "Auntie, this is my friend, Barry, who I wanted you to meet."

"This is the Chocolate Man I wanted you to meet," Ima said.

Barry looked sheepish but shorn.

"Barry, what happened to your hair?" Percy asked.

"I got rid of it."

"How?"

"After you left, I found Droll Troll hiding in a tumbleweed patch. He wanted to be friends with me. And he taught me how to shave."

"Whimsey woo for you," Percy said. "Did you see Tootsie?"

"Droll said she didn't want to meet me."

"Lucky for you," Percy said.

"Then Barry came here to make friends with me and Numen," Ima said. "He's the mysterious stranger who's been dropping off chocolate goodies at my house for years, although I suspected as much. Before, he was afraid to introduce himself to me because he said he looked scary. But I can't see him anyway! Isn't that so funny?!"

Flora shook Barry's hand. "Thanks for helping my nephew," she said. "You know, Barry, I have a theory about the lumps you have on your body. I think it's because you have so much kindness inside you, it bursts out through your skin."

Barry turned pink.

Percy picked up the sleeping pup. "Barry, look what I have. She's a beaut, isn't she?"

Barry's face lit up. "Is that your new dog?"

"No, Barry, she's *your* new dog."

"For me?" Barry held the pup in one hand. "She's a beauty, all right." He gently stroked the puppy's back. "You should see her, Ima."

"I get the picture," Ima said.

"Thank you so—"

"Errf!" The pup woke up and nuzzled Barry's hand.

"She likes you," Percy said.

"What's her name?"

"You name her."

Without hesitation, Barry said, "Angela."

The End